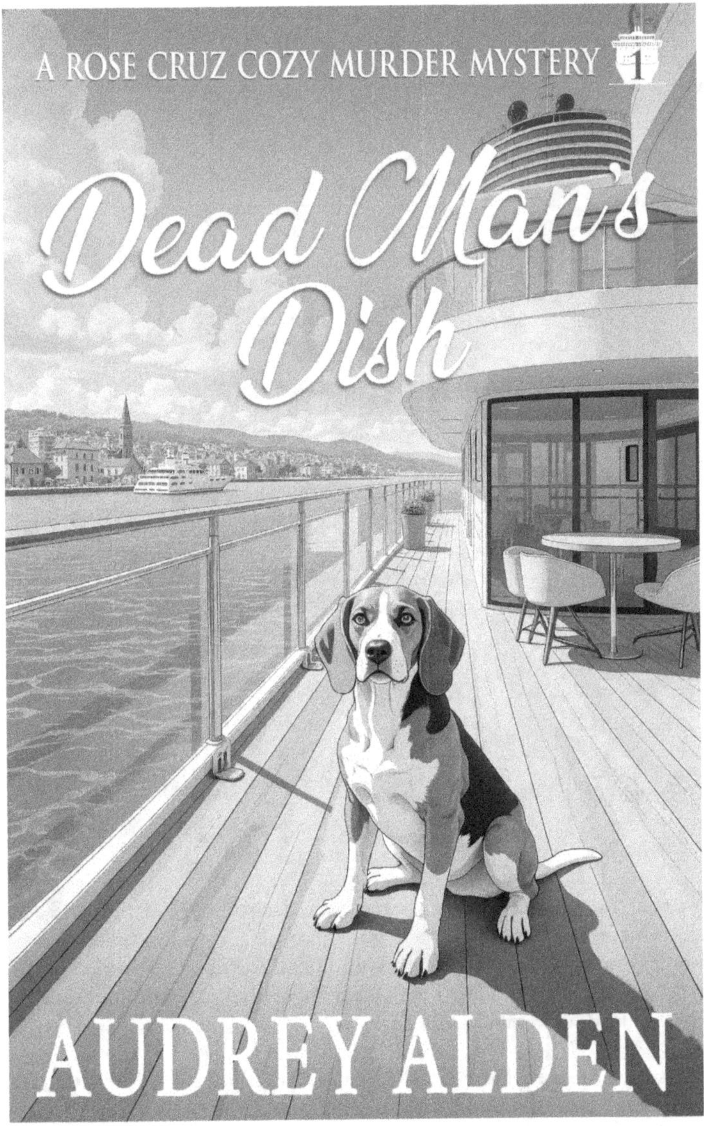

A ROSE CRUZ COZY MURDER MYSTERY

Dead Man's
Dish

AUDREY ALDEN

Contents

Introduction

A luxurious cruise. A high-profile passenger list. And a murder that must be solved before the ship docks.

Rose Dela Cruz thought a change of pace was exactly what she needed. After her career as a private investigator hit a dead end, she accepted a new role as Cruise Director aboard *The Midnight Tide*—seeking peace on the open sea.

But on her first day aboard, tranquility was shattered. Eleanor Bridges, a wealthy and obnoxious guest, was found dead, poisoned during dinner.

With the help of Ben, the ship's captain, Cole, Head of Security, and Rex, her loyal beagle, Rose plunged into a tangled web of suspects. All the alibis were airtight. Everyone seemed innocent—until a second poisoning attempt sent a chilling message: the killer was still onboard.

As Rose followed each lead, she uncovered a network of jealousy, betrayal, and old grudges. But time was running out. With the ship nearing port, the killer was preparing to vanish without a trace.

In a race against time, Rose had to piece together the final pieces of the puzzle—before the truth slipped away forever.

Prologue
Night of the Incident

Please don't be dead. Please don't be dead.

As I shake Eleanor Bridges in her chair, those words loop in my mind like a broken record.

I can already picture the scene if she wakes up—this 65-year-old firecracker will throw a fit, and rightfully so. Her reputation for dramatics precedes her.

It's been a few minutes since I first noticed her head drooping on the table, and I can't help but wonder where her grandson disappeared to. Just moments ago, he was here, animated and chatting with a stunning blonde who left with him.

"Miss Bridges?" I say softly, touching her shoulder and leaning in closer to whisper. "Dinner's almost over. Do you need help back to your suite?"

But she doesn't budge.

I might as well be touching a statue; she feels so still.

Stop it, Rose. I mentally chastise myself.

Dark thoughts have no place in this bright and lively dining hall.

With its glimmering crystal chandeliers, plush carpet, and sweeping windows that frame the vibrant night, this isn't a room meant for the sight of a corpse. It can't be.

Yet, as the seconds tick by and Eleanor remains motionless, my nerves spike. I force myself to breathe, scanning the nearly empty dining hall to make sure no one is close enough to see me press my fingers against the side of her neck.

Yes, I'm checking for a pulse.

I don't want to believe she's dead, but I have to be certain.

With a delicate touch, I position my fingers just below her chin, willing myself to feel a heartbeat beneath her skin.

Nothing.

Oh, god. This can't be happening.

My heart races, faster than it should, but I push back the rising panic. I've encountered dead bodies before—I can't even confirm that Eleanor is dead yet, so I have to stay calm.

Just then, a server approaches our table, and I instinctively turn to intercept him. After all, this has become a crime scene...assuming there is indeed a crime. "I'll take care of this table," I say firmly.

The server nods and backs away. "Got it, Miss Dela Cruz."

Thank goodness.

But the challenge now lies with the remaining twenty-some guests still lingering in the hall.

I need to clear the room without sending anyone into a frenzy.

Maybe, I reason, Eleanor's age is why I can't find a pulse. I gently sweep her silver hair behind her shoulder, trying again.

With my years of training, I should know how to find a pulse. I position my fingers once more, holding my breath as I wait for that reassuring rhythm to calm my anxiety.

But as the silence stretches, it becomes clear that the issue isn't my technique—it's Eleanor's complete lack of a pulse.

That's right; Eleanor Bridges, one of Europe's wealthiest real estate tycoons, is dead in the dining hall of the Midnight Tide.

And I'm the first to discover her body.

This calls for an investigation. Step one: preserve the crime scene.

As the crowd begins to thin, I approach a nearby server, casting glances at Eleanor with every step.

"Excuse me," I tap his shoulder.

He turns, brow furrowed. "Yes, Miss Dela Cruz?"

"Could you please clear the dining hall quickly? And keep it closed?" I note the confusion in his eyes, so I add, "Mrs. Eleanor Bridges is unwell. We need to give her some privacy."

The server glances over my shoulder at Eleanor, who is still slumped over the table.

I hold my breath, anticipating a look of horror. Instead, he nods, saying, "Right away, Miss Dela Cruz."

As he hurries to inform the others, I return to Eleanor's side, desperate to find her awake.

But, of course, she's still motionless.

The servers, on the opposite side of the hall, begin asking the remaining guests to leave, since dinner has concluded.

In mere minutes, the dining hall is cleared, save for the kitchen staff who are busy tidying up.

I can't let anyone discover that Eleanor Bridges is dead, so I take charge. "Everyone, please leave everything as it is and exit the dining hall immediately. We need it empty per...Mrs. Bridges' request."

It's not exactly a lie to speak ill of the dead, is it? This isn't the time for ethical dilemmas.

As my words echo through the hall, the cruise director exchanges puzzled glances with the guests, but eventually, they comply.

Every item in this hall could hold a clue to this unfortunate death—on the very first day of The Dutchman Cruise.

Captain Ben Anderson is going to be frantic.

Before my frustration boils over, I resolve to begin the investigation as soon as I can.

I whip my phone from my suit jacket pocket and dial Ben's number.

He answers immediately. "Rose, how's your first night on the Midnight Tide?"

Habit kicks in, and I almost say everything is going smoothly, but how could I? There's a dead body in our dining hall.

Now that the hall is empty, I let out a long sigh and pinch the bridge of my nose. "Ben, I need you to come to the dining hall. It's... urgent."

A pause stretches out on the line. "Is everything okay?"

"Not really," I admit. "You should see it for yourself."

"Alright. I'll be there."

I hear the rustle of movement on his end, and then I hang up and dial the security chief, Cole Hester.

"Hester here," he answers.

"Mr. Hester, it's Rose Dela Cruz, the cruise director."

"Ms. Dela Cruz," he replies. "What can I do for you?"

I glance back at Eleanor, still lifeless. "You need to come to the dining hall right away."

Minutes later, Ben and Cole step into the dining hall, curiosity etched on their faces.

"Rose," Ben calls as they approach. "What's going on? Why is the dining hall closed?"

My gaze flicks to Eleanor's body, the weight of the moment heavy in the air.

They inch closer, taking in the sight.

Cole's eyes widen as he asks, "Is she...?"

He searches my face for answers, and I nod, feeling a chill settle in my bones. "Unfortunately, she's dead. Eleanor Bridges is dead."

Chapter 1
One Week Before the Incident

Crystal waters shimmer under the Carolina-blue sky—that's the breathtaking view from the café window as I wait for Captain Ben Anderson to arrive.

The sun glistens against the water, enhancing the ripples' dance on the surface, a delightful interplay of wind and waves.

In weather like this, all I want is an iced coffee, so that's exactly what I order while I wait, anticipation buzzing in my chest for Ben and the job offer he's about to present.

It's been three months since his call about a position aboard the Midnight Tide, and after much contemplation, I've decided that giving it a shot is worth it.

Running a private investigation business in Phoenix, Arizona, has proven to be a challenge. Maybe this cruise ship gig is the change I need—who knows where the tide will take me? Pun intended.

The decision is tough, but I settle on a temporary closure of my business rather than shutting down entirely. This way, if things don't work out, I can always return to Phoenix.

Just as my coffee arrives, Captain Ben Anderson strides into the café, looking even more dashing than I remember.

His dark hair is perfectly styled, and his brown eyes sparkle with charm. A bright smile reveals perfect teeth and adds character to his defined jawline. He's dressed in a fitted white polo and light jeans, radiating a handsome appeal that could turn heads anywhere.

"Miss Rose Dela Cruz," he recognizes me immediately as he approaches the table. "Sorry to keep you waiting. After weeks at sea, I had to re-learn how to walk on solid ground."

I laugh at his attempt at humor, even if it's a bit awkward. "That's alright, Captain Anderson. I just arrived myself."

"Ben," he insists, his tone friendly. "Please, just call me Ben. Everyone on the ship calls me Captain Anderson, and I must admit, I miss hearing my first name sometimes."

Though we've only just met, I can already tell Ben has a good-natured personality. He exudes friendliness, likely a necessary trait for someone in his position. After all, the captain should be the most approachable person on board.

I smile, relaxing my stiff posture as if we're not in a job interview. "Alright, Ben. Can I get you something to drink?"

"I'll handle it," he replies with a grin, signaling to a nearby server to order a hot cappuccino despite the warm 75-degree weather.

Once he places his order, he turns back to me. "First, Rose, I hope you don't mind me calling you that. I really appreciate you considering my job offer. I promise you won't regret it."

"Well, I didn't want to pass up the opportunity. So, about this cruise director position, isn't that right? What does it entail exactly?"

"The contract I sent you was a bit on the lengthy side, wasn't it?" He gives a soft smile. "In a nutshell, you'll be the face of the Midnight Tide. You'll be on the ground, making announcements, introducing activities, and overseeing entertainment. It sounds challenging, doesn't it?"

Although his summary is much less daunting than the formal contract, it still feels a bit outside my wheelhouse.

I wrinkle my nose, skepticism creeping in. "I don't quite understand why you'd want me for that position. It seems like you need someone with more experience in... management."

"Don't you? I heard you run your own business."

"It's a small company," I explain.

"Same difference," he grins, flashing his charming smile. "Plus, the cruise director is responsible for passenger security and safety. I couldn't think of anyone better suited for that role than you."

Thinking back to my first experience on the Midnight Tide, I can see how I might have left that impression. Maybe his job offer does make some sense after all.

Plus, it pays well.

I exhale, feeling the weight of the decision lift. "Alright, when do I start?"

If I thought Ben's smile couldn't get any bigger, I was wrong. "Would you say you're 'on board'?"

I chuckle at his pun. "Aye, aye, Captain."

After the playful banter and half a cup of coffee later, we turn our focus to business.

Ben begins, "So listen, Rose, I wanted to meet before we set sail because I need your help looking into some security agencies."

I blink, recalling the last incompetent agency we worked with. "Is that so? Sure."

Ben powers up his tablet and scrolls through it briefly before handing it to me. "I've gathered some of the best security agencies in Amsterdam, and I need your expertise to decide who to hire."

"Let's take a look." I examine the e-documents on the screen. "Have you met with any of these companies yet?"

"No, not yet," he replies. "We just arrived in port yesterday, so I haven't made any appointments. I figured a private investigator would know more about safety and security than I do."

"Oh, don't flatter me too much, Ben. I might get used to it."

"You should because I'll treat you well," he leans forward slightly, studying my face as if trying to read my reaction—or perhaps watching the pink blush rise to my cheeks.

I shift my attention back to the tablet, poring over their portfolios and proposals even as he waits in a patient silence.

He hired me for my work ethic, didn't he?

I skim the pages until I identify three appealing offers. "Let's set up interviews with Prime Security, Maximillian, and Soteria Safety."

I slide the tablet back to him, and he accepts it, intrigued. "Why those three?"

"Well, Prime Security has worked with some of the top-rated hotels in Amsterdam, which speaks volumes. Maximillian is new but eager, willing to send their best employees, including a former security officer from a cargo ship company."

I glance up to ensure he's following my explanation. "And Soteria has the longest history in the business."

"If you had to choose one agency, who would it be?"

"I won't make that call until I've spoken with their representatives."

"How about tonight?"

"Tonight? What do you mean?"

Ben's smirk returns, almost flirtatious, leading me to wonder if I'm imagining things.

He replies, "How about we sit down for dinner tonight?"

My heart leaps into my throat.

Is he asking me out on a...date? Or am I reading too much into this?

Then Ben chuckles, dispelling my confusion. "I mean, to discuss these security agencies."

"Oh..." I nearly misunderstood him; thankfully, I pause before saying anything rash. "Y-yeah, of course. It's part of the job, right?"

As I get ready for dinner, I wonder if my outfit is appropriate for the occasion. It wasn't intentional—I thought a chiffon blouse and jeans would suffice for a business dinner. But seeing Ben makes me rethink my choice.

I don't even think he made an effort.

"Am I too casual?" I blurt as I join him at our table; he insists I sit beside him for the meetings with the security companies tonight.

So, I do.

Being this close to him offers an intoxicating whiff of his cologne.

Ben smiles at me. "No, you look great. I just enjoy dressing up whenever I'm off the ship. Don't worry about it."

"Oh, okay," I reply, perusing the menu.

We decide on a seafood course for dinner.

As the salad is served, Ben says, "You know what, Rose? I lied. We're not meeting with three representatives today. I chose one of your picks to speed things up."

I stab my romaine lettuce with my fork, intrigued. "Is that so? That's fine by me, as long as you think he's a good fit."

"I went with Maximillian; their cargo ship guy turns out to be a 'local hero.' Saved a few lives on his ship back in the day. I think he'll be a great addition to our team."

"Really? What kind of heroic things has he done?"

Ben gestures toward the entrance of the restaurant. "You can ask him yourself. Here he comes."

A guy who resembles a real-life Peter Pan strides toward our table, looking to be in his thirties.

He has tousled blonde hair, bright green eyes, and a friendly smile that makes him look innocent. "Captain Ben Anderson?"

Ben rises to shake his hand. "That's me. And this is the Midnight Tide's cruise director, Rose Dela Cruz."

Not officially, I almost add. Instead, I extend my hand. "Hello there, Mr....?"

"Cole Hester," he introduces himself. "I've heard of you, Ms. Dela Cruz. I read about how you cracked the case of Dr. Robert Franz on the Midnight Tide."

I can't suppress my smile; I had no idea there was even an article about my first case. "Oh, please, don't flatter me."

Ben interjects, "Alright, you two, let's have a seat. I'm starving."

We all sit and begin to enjoy dinner while casually getting to know Cole Hester.

I'm the first to ask him, "Captain Anderson mentioned you were a hero on your previous cargo ship. What experiences do you have, if you don't mind sharing?"

Cole looks down at his plate, a hint of shyness creeping into his demeanor. "Oh, it's nothing impressive. I was just looking after a few of my fellow crew members, that's all."

Ben nudges me, adopting a conspiratorial whisper that Cole can still hear. "He caught a massive drug operation aboard their cargo ship, saved an old man from cardiac arrest, and even rescued a junior engineer from falling overboard."

I can't hide my surprise as I turn my gaze to Cole. "That's... quite impressive. And here you are, downplaying it, Mr. Hester."

He smiles sincerely, a hint of embarrassment coloring his cheeks. "I was just doing my job, really."

Ben leans in, his enthusiasm palpable. "And that's exactly the kind of attitude we want on the Midnight Tide. Of course, if you're interested in accepting our offer."

Cole's face lights up. "If you want me to work with you, Captain, I'd be thrilled. It would be a pleasure."

"What do you think, Rose?" Ben turns to me with an expectant look.

Though Cole and I have only just met, his humility and kindness reveal much about his character. His impressive background makes him an attractive candidate for the role, and I'd love to have someone like him on board.

I nod at Ben, feeling a sense of excitement. "I think I'd enjoy working with Mr. Hester."

"Fantastic!" Ben exclaims, grinning from ear to ear. "Welcome aboard, Cole!"

The three of us continue to eat, the atmosphere lightening as we share stories about our experiences at sea. I find myself relaxing more with each passing moment, enjoying the camaraderie.

As dessert is served—a decadent chocolate mousse—I take a moment to observe Cole and Ben. They seem to share a natural rapport, which bodes well for the team dynamics on the Midnight Tide.

"So, Cole, what's your favorite part about working on a ship?" I ask, genuinely curious.

He leans back, considering my question. "Honestly? The unpredictability. Every day is different, and you never know what kind of adventure is waiting around the corner."

I smile, picturing all the potential scenarios. "I can see how that would be exciting. I think I'll have my share of surprises as well."

Ben nods, clearly pleased. "That's the spirit! With you two on board, I feel more confident about the upcoming voyage. We'll make an excellent team."

With dessert finished and the conversation flowing easily, I feel a sense of camaraderie forming between us. It's refreshing, especially after the loneliness of running my own business.

As we wrap up our dinner, Ben leans in, a more serious tone taking over. "Rose, I want you to know that I have high hopes for this cruise. With your skills and Cole's experience, we can tackle any challenges that come our way."

"Challenges? What do you mean?" I ask, my curiosity piqued.

He glances around as if gauging the atmosphere before answering. "You never know what might happen on a cruise. Accidents, security threats—things can get complicated."

Cole nods in agreement, his expression turning more serious. "It's essential to have a good team ready to handle any situation."

I swallow hard, the gravity of the job sinking in. "I understand. I'm ready for it."

Ben smiles, his confidence infectious. "That's what I like to hear. Together, we'll ensure the Midnight Tide is safe and enjoyable for everyone on board."

As we finish our meal, I can't help but feel a mix of excitement and nerves. This could be the start of something significant, both in my career and in my life.

After we settle the bill, we make our way out of the restaurant, stepping into the cool evening air. The bustling sounds of the city surround us, and for a moment, I feel a sense of belonging.

"Are you ready for this, Rose?" Ben asks, glancing at me with a hint of concern.

"Absolutely," I reply, my heart racing. "Let's get this journey started."

And just like that, the Midnight Tide feels like more than just a cruise ship; it feels like a new beginning.

Chapter 2
Two Days Before the Incident

"Rosie!" My sister, Stacy Dela Cruz, squeals as she spots me waiting for her in the airport's arrival area in Amsterdam.

My ever-supportive sister agrees to fly back to Amsterdam to join me on the Midnight Tide for its latest cruise, dubbed "The Dutchman Cruise."

It's a 15-day journey from Amsterdam to Ireland.

She rushes towards me, enveloping me in a tight hug as if she hasn't seen me in ages, though it's only been five days since I left Phoenix. "How have you been!?"

I can't help but laugh at her enthusiasm. "Oh, come on, don't act like we haven't been talking on the phone every single day."

Her jet-black hair, just like mine, sways in rhythm with her as we walk shoulder to shoulder. "You know, I just miss you all the time. Phoenix isn't the same without you."

"Says the girl who travels constantly for work," I tease.

"It's an occupational hazard." Stacy grins, looping her arm through mine. "So, how did your meeting with Captain Anderson go?"

"It's great, I think," I reply, smiling as I recall our conversation. "We hired a security agency together and—"

"And you're blushing!" Stacy gasps. "Oh my god, do you like Captain Anderson? I mean, I won't judge! He's a total cutie."

"Stace!" I exclaim, still getting used to her lack of subtlety. "It's nothing like that. I just think he's... a nice guy, that's all."

"Nice? That's like giving a restaurant three stars. 'Service is slow, but I can wait,' or 'Food is bland, but that's what salt shakers are for.' We both know Captain Anderson offers top-notch service and is quite the appetizer."

I playfully hit her arm. "Oh my god, you're going to make a big deal out of this, aren't you?"

"Only because I can spot a crush when I see one. And you definitely have a crush on Captain—"

I cover my ears and sprint away from her, heading towards the parking area where my rental car is waiting.

I hear Stacy laughing behind me as she drags her suitcase along.

Once inside the car, she buckles her seatbelt as I start the engine. "I'm still feeling pretty jet-lagged from the flight. How about we visit Albert Cuyp Market later this afternoon? For now, let's watch movies and order lunch at the hotel."

"Alright," I smile, backing out of the parking space. "I'm all yours for today."

"You better be; I didn't fly 6,000 miles for nothing."

"Oh, don't be so dramatic. You're going to be with me for the next 15 days on the Midnight Tide."

"Despite that, it's never enough."

Stacy and I drive back to the hotel, following her wishes.

In a sisterly tradition, we indulge in a cheesy romantic comedy while devouring pizza, nachos, and a celebratory bottle of champagne at one in the afternoon. Stacy insists it's to toast my new job.

We only pour two glasses, mindful to stay sober for the rest of the afternoon, especially since I need to meet the crew on the cruise ship later tonight.

By four o'clock, Stacy and I head to Albert Cuyp Market, a long stretch of stalls bustling with vibrant items and delicious foods.

Of course, we seize the chance to try their local kippeling, stroopwafels, and grilled cheese.

Stacy even picks up a few souvenirs for her co-workers.

After a satisfying stroll through the lively market, we make our way to the infamous Anne Frank House.

Since we're in Amsterdam, it seems only fitting, right?

As our tour begins, I lean over to Stacy and whisper, "Dead people receive more flowers than the living because regret is stronger than gratitude."

Stacy gives me a puzzled look. "Jesus, that's dark. Just say if you want flowers, and I'll make sure to tell Captain Anderson."

"Stacy!" I scold her, trying to hold back laughter. "It's an Anne Frank quote."

"It felt more like a quote for Ben, my brother-in-law."

I laugh again; Stacy has a real talent for taking jokes way too far. I'm used to her humor.

She'll tire of it soon enough.

Plus, I honestly don't mind the teasing about Ben; I take it as a compliment.

We wander through the museum and take a leisurely stroll around the neighborhood surrounding Anne Frank's home.

After a fun-filled afternoon, we decide to call it a day.

Back at the hotel, Stacy kicks off her shoes and flops onto the bed. "I'm so tired. What do you feel like having for dinner? I'm thinking salmon."

I walk straight to the closet, shrugging off my cardigan while searching for something more professional to wear. "I told you I have to meet the crew and staff of the Midnight Tide. We're having a welcome dinner."

Stacy sits up with a pout. "Can I come?"

"I'd love for you to join, but it's a crew and staff-only event. Sorry."

"I knew I should've quit my job and applied to the Midnight Tide!"

If anyone saw her, they'd think she was the younger sibling, so I chuckle. "Don't worry; you're my guest on the cruise. You're practically a VIP."

"That's what I'm talking about!"

I turn back to my closet and settle on a white and black striped jacket, but then Stacy asks, "Is that what you're wearing to your 'company' dinner?"

I haven't even slipped my arm into the sleeve. "Um, yes...?"

"Uh-uh," Stacy hops off the bed and drags her luggage over to me. "I won't let you wear that lousy thing to dinner. That jacket doesn't scream 'cruise director.'"

I glance down at one of my favorite work jackets. "I don't think there's a need to dress up. It's fine—"

"Just listen to me this time, Rose; you're going to regret not dressing up when you get there."

Then, she pulls out a peach-colored dress from her pile of clothes. "Now, this is the winner. Wear it."

I look at it in horror.

While Stacy and I are practically the same size, our tastes in clothing are worlds apart. She loves being seen—and it's not a bad thing. Meanwhile, I prefer to blend into the background.

But I know from experience that I'll lose this argument with Stacy, so I reluctantly put the dress on.

I almost hate how well it fits. It's a long-sleeved, body-wrap dress with a V-neckline. I fix my eyes on it, frowning. "I couldn't possibly wear this; I can see my... assets in this."

"Hardly!" Stacy retorts, tugging the hem of the dress down below my knees. "I think it looks like you've 'girl-bossed' too hard, and now you're a cruise director. Respect can come in a pretty package, you know?"

"I think they'd respect me even if I'm not wearing this dress."

"They'll respect you more," Stacy insists, wrapping her arms around me for a quick hug. "Now, you're a size seven in shoes, right? I have the perfect heels for that."

I feel surprisingly confident in Stacy's clothes and shoes, so I must thank her for dressing me for dinner on the Midnight Tide.

As soon as I board the ship, friendly faces take me in, their smiles welcoming.

At the entrance, Ben stands in his captain's uniform, speaking to a few others in semi-formal attire.

Seeing their outfits, I'm grateful Stacy made the right call.

As I approach, Ben catches sight of me and does a double take. Then he beams. "Miss Rose Dela Cruz, welcome aboard."

I smile back, feeling the urge to tug my dress down, which rides up slightly with each step. "Captain Anderson, thank you for having me."

Ben turns to the well-dressed individuals beside him. "Rose, this is Warren and Kellie, the hotel directors, and Michael Sutton, the chief engineer."

They all shake my hand as I introduce myself. "Hello, I'm Rose Dela Cruz."

Ben adds, "She's the new cruise director for the Midnight Tide."

He places a hand on the small of my back, guiding me forward in the most chivalrous way. "Everyone, let's head to the dining hall for dinner."

Then he leans in and murmurs, "You're going to meet a crowd of people here, so I hope you're ready to remember all their names."

"Does everyone know each other?"

"Quite a few," Ben replies. "But since the launch of 'The Dutchman Cruise,' we've had a bit of a restructuring."

I take a moment to soak in the ship as if it's my first visit.

Arriving at the dining hall, the sweeping ocean views through the windows still take my breath away. Then, I shift my attention to Ben, who is introducing me to the chief doctor and the staff captain.

There are just so many people on board the Midnight Tide.

Almost a hundred if I'm keeping count.

As Ben engages in conversation with everyone, I'm relieved to spot Cole sitting by himself at a nearby table.

I walk over, a smile breaking across my face. "Mr. Hester, you're here."

"Miss Dela Cruz," he replies with a warm smile. "It's quite overwhelming, trying to get to know everyone, huh?"

"I know. I think I've heard twenty names already, and none of them stick."

Cole chuckles. "Glad to see a familiar face in the crowd."

Just then, Ben approaches me as the soup is being served around the tables. "Rose, hey, could you join me for a second?"

I nod, excusing myself from Cole.

To my surprise, Ben leads me to the front of the dining hall, where he retrieves a microphone and calls for everyone's attention. "Everyone, good evening! I'm thrilled to have you all aboard the Midnight Tide for our welcome dinner."

The room erupts in applause as I stand awkwardly beside him, a bit overwhelmed by the attention.

He continues, "Since our cruise ship has taken an improved route with 'The Dutchman Cruise,' we've made some changes in our management team. First and foremost, I'd like to introduce the newest member of our ship."

He gestures for me to step closer, and I do so, my heart pounding.

Ben speaks into the microphone. "You may remember her from one of our previous cruises three months ago as the woman who solved the case of Dr. Robert Franz. Thankfully, I've managed to convince her to join us. Everyone, a round of applause for Ms. Rose Dela Cruz, the new cruise director of the Midnight Tide."

A warm wave of applause washes over me, a mix of welcoming cheers and friendly faces.

Standing before this crowd of unknown yet friendly people fills me with a rare sense of honor.

As I smile back at them, I feel an overwhelming sense of belonging. I'm excited for the adventure ahead.

I can't shake the feeling that I'm going to cherish every moment of this cruise.

Here's to hoping our journey goes smoothly.

Chapter 3
Fourteen Hours Before the Incident

"Are you nervous?" Ben joins me at the end of the gangway, the walkway connecting the dock to the ship where all the passengers board.

I smooth down my pencil skirt with my hands. "A little, yes. I don't know how to greet the guests."

Ben chuckles as he stands beside me, his hands clasped in front of him. "Just say, 'Welcome to The Dutchman Cruise.' You don't have to sing for them… at least, not yet."

"What?" I exclaim, momentarily fooled into thinking I might have to perform for the guests.

"I'm just kidding," he winks at me.

Just then, Ben's first mate approaches. "Everything's in order, Captain."

"Great," Ben replies. "Inform the crew that we're ready for the passengers."

"Got it, Captain."

The first mate pulls out his radio and relays the order. With each passing second, my nerves ramp up; it's not like I have prior experience dealing with five hundred passengers.

That's right, five hundred. I scanned the list of passengers they gave me last night.

As we stand at the frontline, a few other crew members join us, and soon, people begin to stroll up the gangway.

Ben calls out to me one last time, gesturing to my crooked nametag, and I quickly fix it, muttering a thank you.

Finally, the passengers start boarding the vessel, one after another.

I plaster on my best smile, welcoming them to the Midnight Tide's inaugural Dutchman Cruise.

Some guests recognize Ben, shaking his hand as they pass us.

After about fifteen minutes, my cheeks are starting to feel numb from all the smiling.

A young gentleman walks up the deck alongside a presumably older woman, and Ben nods at me, urging me to follow him. So, I do.

Ben assists the older woman, who sports pearls around her neck and several gold and diamond rings on her fingers. "Mrs. Eleanor Bridges, it seems you've finally unlocked the secret to reverse aging."

Eleanor Bridges? I recall her name from the list.

That means her companion must be... Dale Bridges!

They're among our VIPs on board.

I step forward to greet the younger man, taking Ben's cue. "Mr. Dale Bridges, welcome to the Midnight Tide. Is this your first time on board?"

Dale beams at me, his blue eyes sparkling—maybe reflecting the sea itself. "Oh, no. We've been here every year for the last five years. My grandmother loves her cruises."

"That's wonderful to hear," I respond. "I believe you'll have a fantastic time."

"We always do."

Ben chimes in, "Dale, Eleanor, this is Rose Dela Cruz. She's the ship's new cruise director."

Eleanor gives me a bored glance before returning her attention to Ben. "You hired a young cruise director? Does she even have enough experience to handle your passengers?"

It feels as if she's addressing me as if I'm invisible. If Stacy were here, she would have certainly taken offense.

Where is she, anyway?

Ben reassures her, "Oh, Eleanor, she's the best I could ever hope for. You'll be amazed at all the wonders she has planned for the passengers. You're going to love her."

Eleanor grunts in response.

Dale leans closer to me and whispers, "Don't worry about her; she has something against young women. I think she's just jealous that time has caught up to her."

I chuckle politely. "Don't worry about me, Mr. Bridges."

"Oh, I'm not," he glances at his grandmother. "I'm more concerned about her. Jealousy doesn't look good on anyone."

Except Eleanor Bridges doesn't have a reason to be jealous.

Even with her age, she carries herself beautifully, dressed elegantly for the occasion. Her silver hair complements her fair complexion.

Ben and I escort the VIP guests to their suite before excusing ourselves.

Ben offers a temporary goodbye. "We'll come back once you've settled in, Eleanor. I'll see you in a few minutes."

As we walk down the hallway, retracing our steps, Ben chats, "Did you know Eleanor Bridges is one of the wealthiest real estate tycoons in Europe? Her family owns a massive hotel franchise."

"Seems like it," I remark. "She's wearing enough jewelry to feed an entire family for a year."

"A decade," Ben corrects me with a gentle smile. "But don't worry, she'll warm up to you. Once she does, you'll find she's one of the most amiable women you'll ever meet."

"Really?"

Ben snorts. "No. She's what people would call a 'prima donna.' But you'll get used to it."

I laugh. "Is that supposed to make me feel better? Because it's not working."

Before Ben can respond, a woman's voice calls out to him. "If it isn't Captain Ben Anderson."

Ben turns toward the voice, and a stunning, tall woman with blonde hair and striking green eyes approaches, giving Ben a friendly hug.

Ben hugs her back. "Allison Rye, as I live and breathe. How have you been?"

"I'm well," Allison replies, her red lipstick bright against her smile. "I was thrilled to receive your invitation to The Dutchman Cruise. I've missed the ocean."

"The city's treating you well, I hope?"

"You know I won't brag, but you could say that."

"Great," Ben says, turning to me. "Allison, by the way, this is Rose Dela Cruz. She's our cruise director."

I'm being introduced a lot, but I suppose my job requires that people know who I am—who to call if they ever need anything.

I extend my hand for a shake, but Allison surprises me by kissing me cheek-to-cheek.

Allison playfully teases Ben, "You have a knack for attracting beautiful women like us, Captain Anderson."

"Right." Ben laughs, shaking his head. "Allison was the ship's head chef until she was... poached. I should know who your new employer is."

Allison rolls her eyes. "I'd tell you if I could, but you know, NDA."

"If you say so," Ben replies.

"I wouldn't lie to you, you know."

I sense a long-standing friendship between Ben and Allison. My instincts as a private investigator tell me there's a deep ease between them, but it feels strictly platonic.

Not that I care if it ever was romantic—of course not.

Ben says to Allison, "Well, we better get back to work. See you around, Al."

"See ya, Captain," Allison smiles at me. "You too, Rose."

I return the smile. "Of course, you better be at the dining hall tonight. I have a show prepared for the passengers."

Allison nods enthusiastically. "I'll be there!"

As I catch up to Ben's long strides, I say, "She's nice. And pretty, too."

"She is," Ben agrees. "Speaking of shows tonight, we should probably part ways for now. I'm sure you have your hands full on the first day of the cruise."

"That I do."

"I'll see you later, Rose."

"See you too, Captain."

As we separate, a sudden commotion erupts from Eleanor's suite, prompting us to return to the hallway.

We find Eleanor splashing water on a server's face.

Eleanor yells, "Do you even know the difference between lukewarm and room temperature water, you imbecile?"

Dale steps in, his voice calm but firm. "Grandma, please, that's too much."

Eleanor pulls her arm away from Dale's grasp. "Oh, no. What's too much is not listening to my preferences!"

I'm mortified—but the female server is even more so. She stands frozen in the middle of the room, tears welling up in her eyes.

Ben isn't pleased either, but he holds back, stepping inside the suite. "Eleanor, is everything okay?"

"Oh, Captain Anderson," Eleanor visibly relaxes at his presence. "I'm just concerned your staff needs a bit more training."

Ben looks at me, nodding at the server, and I step forward to lead her out of the suite by the shoulders.

I hand her my handkerchief. "Are you okay?"

The server shakily accepts it. "I'm... okay. Thank you," she replies.

"I'm really sorry about that," I tell her. "I'm sure Captain Anderson won't let this slide."

"No, it's okay, ma'am," she insists, her voice cracking as she fights back tears. "It happens sometimes."

But it shouldn't, I almost argue.

The server finishes wiping her face before finally excusing herself. "I'll change for now. Thank you for getting me out of there, Miss Dela Cruz."

Chapter 4
Two Hours Before the Incident

I flop down on the mattress in my quarters. Unlike the crew deck, I have an entire room to myself, complete with a closet and a small table with a chair.

There's even a cozy nook in the corner for Rex, my beagle. At least, that's what we've agreed upon—he and I are partners now.

Thank you, Robert.

As always, Rex is out wandering the halls, but I'm not worried; he always manages to find me.

Stacy surveys my half-empty bedroom. "It's a nice room, despite the lack of windows."

"The last thing I need right now is a window." I close my eyes for a moment. "I need to rest."

I feel Stacy walking around the room. "It's only 6:30 in the evening. I think you rest when the passengers rest."

"I know," I sigh. "I should've seen this coming, considering the pay is high."

Since eight in the morning, I've been working non-stop. I only had a thirty-minute break after lunch, and that was it.

I've greeted and assisted passengers, prepared the welcome video during lunch, had a quick meeting with Cole and his team, and made sure my performers for tonight were ready. It's nothing like running my private investigation firm.

The mattress shifts as Stacy sits at the edge of the bed. She touches my arm, prompting me to look at her. "I think you're doing great, Rose."

"Of course you do," I sit up. "Even my breathing is amazing to you."

"It's because you're my sister!"

"I know." I squeeze her hand. "Thanks for always supporting me."

"You'd do the same for me, anyway."

Stacy stands up from the bed and extends her hand. "Break time is over, Miss Dela Cruz. Dinner preparations are in order."

I groan dramatically.

"On it, Miss Dela Cruz."

Before leaving the room, I fill Rex's bowl with food and fresh water, then we're off.

I'm grateful Stacy is here on the ship with me. While she can't officially help out, she makes an effort to cheer me up instead of just enjoying her 15-day vacation. I appreciate that about her.

We head to the kitchen together, where I review the menu one more time.

Today's five-course dinner includes Dutch Oven Minestrone Soup, Watermelon Salad with Feta and Mint, Shrimp Tartlets, Clams in Sorrel Garlic Cream, and Tart Meyer Lemon Sorbet.

Compliments to the chef, indeed.

After confirming that everything is in order, I wander through the dining hall. Stacy is now busy on her phone, likely talking to one of her company's executives.

As I move around the hall, I adjust folded napkins and check glasses and utensils. But doing that for five hundred people feels tedious, so I'm relieved when Kellie, the hotel director, joins me for the final touches before dinner.

"Tell me a secret," Kellie says as we check the tables. "Is it true you got the Dutch National Ballet to perform at tonight's dinner?"

I can't help but smile. "Rumors travel fast, don't they?"

"So it's true! That's impressive! I was expecting the usual live music for the first night."

"Oh, well, I wanted to make a great impression."

"Well, I'm excited!"

By seven in the evening, we finally open the dining hall.

Along with Kellie, I help the guests find their seats, ensuring everyone is comfortable and has an unobstructed view of the center of the dining area, where I've arranged for the performers to dance.

We have to adjust a few tables, but I think it's worth it.

By 7:30, most of the guests are seated in the dining hall. Even Eleanor and Dale Bridges are present, seemingly engaged in a heated discussion.

Perhaps they're discussing Eleanor's unbecoming behavior from earlier. I can't help but wonder how that girl is doing now.

I hope she didn't take Eleanor's words too much to heart.

I scan the room for Ben and Allison, but neither of them is here yet.

Since Ben is the ship's captain, I can't hold his absence against him.

Not wanting to waste any more time, I position myself in the center of the room with a microphone. "Good evening, ladies and gentlemen. On the first night of The

Dutchman Cruise, we've arranged a viewing experience of Amsterdam's arts unlike any other."

I'm really nervous; I hope no one can tell.

I continue, "With that in mind, I'd like to call on the Dutch National Ballet to perform for us tonight. Let's give them a warm welcome."

The crowd erupts into cheers and applause as the graceful ballerinas glide into the center of the room, taking their positions just as they rehearsed earlier this afternoon.

I step aside, signaling to the technical guy to dim the lights.

Finally, the music starts.

In perfect unison, the ballerinas move even more smoothly than Captain Anderson steering the ship.

Their skirts flow with every movement; their arms and legs work together in the most beautiful dance imaginable.

Delicate yet powerful—that's how I would describe it.

I look around and find Stacy giving me a thumbs-up. It relieves me to see her and everyone else enjoying the dinner performance.

After their ten-minute routine, the cheers and applause ring loud and clear.

Good job, Rose. I tell myself.

As dinner begins, I stand off to the side, watching the servers bring meals to the tables.

Seeing the passengers smile, laugh, and relish their time fills me with a sense of satisfaction.

This job is surprisingly rewarding.

By the time dessert is served, Allison finally appears in the dining hall.

She spots me immediately and rushes over, a bit out of breath. "Rose, hi! I'm so sorry to have missed the performance. I overslept."

"Oh, no, it's alright!" I assure her. "You have 14 more nights to enjoy."

"Great! I'm looking forward to it."

"Sure. How about I find a table for you—"

"Oh, no," Allison interrupts me. "Don't worry about it. I can do that myself."

"Are you sure?"

"Oh, please. I know this dining hall like the back of my hand."

With a little wave, Allison sets off to find a table.

I can't help but smile at how nice she is—like a pocketful of sunshine.

While watching her, I notice she accidentally bumps into Dale, and they immediately engage in conversation.

It's no surprise; they're both good-looking people—one came alone, and the other is with his grandma.

The potential for romance is blooming.

Trying not to meddle in anyone's business, even if it's just watching too closely, I spend the next half hour mingling with passengers, gathering their feedback about the performance and the food.

Both are receiving wonderful comments.

At one point, I sit down with Stacy, who is also enjoying herself.

Just as I leave Stacy's table to greet the departing guests, I spot Allison and Dale walking out of the dining hall together, navigating through the thinning crowd.

They're laughing and chatting, clearly hitting it off.

I smile to myself as I watch them disappear from the hall. Instinctively, I scan the area for Eleanor, wondering if I've missed her already.

In a space this wide, navigating through five hundred people can be challenging.

Thankfully, I find her after a few seconds of searching.

As I approach her table, I realize Eleanor is sleeping, her back slumped and head down.

Is she okay? I wonder to myself as I quicken my pace.

Her position looks uncomfortable—almost unnatural. So unnatural that a sense of worry creeps in.

As I draw closer, Eleanor's image sharpens.

Her position suggests one of two things: she's either fallen asleep or... she's dead.

Chapter 5

Fifteen Minutes After the Incident

"She's dead?" Cole repeats my words, his face a mix of disbelief and concern. "What do you mean, she's dead?"

I wish I didn't have to be the one to confirm it. "She has no pulse; she hasn't moved at all."

Cole does a double-take before stepping closer, pointing toward Eleanor. "May I check for myself?"

I nod. "Go ahead."

Ben and I watch Cole closely as he mimics my earlier actions, placing two fingers under Eleanor's chin in search of a pulse.

When Cole can't find it either, he frantically tries the other side of her neck and then her wrists.

The color drains from Cole's face as he takes a step back from Eleanor.

Shaking his head at Ben, he confirms, "She has no pulse, Captain."

Ben goes quiet for a moment, his expression shifting from shock to concern. Finally, he lets out a shaky breath. "How—how did this happen?"

I almost feel the urge to blame myself, but this is no time for that. Rationally speaking, there's no way I can look after five hundred passengers.

So, I answer Ben calmly, "Do you know if Eleanor has a history of... strokes? Maybe a heart attack?"

"No," Ben shakes his head. "For all I know, she's a healthy woman. But I haven't seen her in months, and anything could've happened since then. We should ask Dale."

Ben scans the empty dining hall. "Where is he, by the way?"

"He left earlier with Allison," I reply.

"Allison Rye?"

"Yes."

Ben focuses intently on Eleanor. "How was Dale when he left? Could he have known Eleanor... is dead?"

"No, I don't think so. Dale was smiling and laughing when he left."

"We should tell him."

Cole chimes in. "Just him, right? We have to keep this under wraps for now; no one can find out about this. Everyone in this dining hall is a suspect... if there's foul play involved."

I couldn't agree more. "That's right. We don't want the passengers to panic, either. I realized that earlier, so I had everyone leave and closed the dining hall for privacy. For now, it's just the three of us who know."

Ben looks as if he's in shock, staring blankly at Eleanor's lifeless body.

Then he exhales deeply. "Alright, then. Let's agree to keep quiet about this. For now, I'll call the medical examiner onboard to determine the cause of death. Maybe we can have an autopsy performed since we'll be at sea for a while."

"Okay," I croak. "Cole and I will take photos of the crime scene and gather as much evidence as we can."

Cole's expression shifts to surprise and confusion, giving away his inexperience. This must be his first time dealing with a dead body on board.

Maybe even a murder.

I hope not.

Ben steps out of the hall to call and brief the medical examiner. Meanwhile, Cole stands frozen.

I gently touch his arm. "Hey, it's alright. If you need to sit down, it's okay with me. I can handle this myself."

"N-no," Cole takes a deep breath. "I'll help. Just tell me what you need me to do."

"Are you sure?"

"Yes. I'm the head of security, and this is part of my duty."

"Okay, then." I admire Cole's dedication. "Um, we need something like a sealable plastic bag to store evidence from this table."

Cole looks around, his eyes landing on the kitchen, where the lights are still on. "Okay, got it."

"I'll take some photos for now."

"Okay, I'll be right back."

Cole jogs toward the kitchen, leaving me alone with Eleanor in the dining hall. I whip my phone out and start taking multiple photos of the crime scene, almost feeling sorry for what I'm doing to Eleanor.

But someone has to do it; this ship has no detectives, and we're still days away from port.

So, for now, I capture images of Eleanor in her chair.

I photograph the table—the glasses, utensils, and plates. I document her surroundings, too, including the floors and the empty chair that Dale occupied earlier.

I make sure to include Dale's side of the table in the photos.

Cole is the first to return. He hands me some plastic bags, and we use tissue paper between our fingers as we pick up the items from the table.

He also brings an empty box for us to store everything inside.

Midway through our task, the dining hall door swings open—Ben enters with a man in his sixties, wheeling a chair behind him.

"Everyone, this is Dr. Monty Bates. He's the ship's medical examiner," Ben introduces him, his tone lacking enthusiasm. "Monty, this is Rose and Cole."

Dr. Bates nods at us, his gaze fixed on Eleanor like a moth drawn to a flame.

He pushes the wheelchair closer to Eleanor's body. "We're going to have to move her to the morgue. But to avoid panic, we need to make it look like a medical emergency. We won't use a body bag or stretcher for now."

It seems like a sensible plan—anyone seeing us wheeling Eleanor would assume she's merely unwell.

Dr. Bates pulls some latex gloves from his pockets and approaches Eleanor for an initial assessment.

He lifts her chin, exposing her face—eyes closed, mouth slightly ajar, as if caught in a frown.

"She's still warm," Dr. Bates states. "She just died, didn't she?"

I reply, "Fifteen to twenty minutes, tops."

Dr. Bates continues to examine Eleanor, speaking almost to himself. "I'm not seeing any visible wounds—no blood or anything. Since the victim just died, it's hard to determine anything without conducting an autopsy."

He studies Eleanor's face more closely, opening her eyes with his fingers. "Hmm, a bit of dilation in her conjunctiva. My first guess would be myocardial infarction."

Heart attack, I think to myself.

Given how quickly the minutes passed, I would also surmise Eleanor passed from something sudden, like a heart attack.

But I'm no expert in that area.

Dr. Bates steps back from Eleanor's body and removes his gloves. He turns to Cole. "If you can, please carefully place her body in this wheelchair so we can transport her to the morgue."

I can see Cole is uncomfortable; the lines on his forehead deepen. Still, he complies.

Quickly, Ben lends a hand.

They ease Eleanor's body from the chair into the wheelchair. As they do, I stabilize the wheelchair.

Cole takes the handle from my grip and follows Dr. Bates out of the hall.

Ben speaks, "We should talk to Dale; inform him of our situation. He'll likely get worried if his grandmother doesn't return to their suite soon."

I pick up the box of evidence Cole and I collected. "I'll take this to my room for safekeeping, then I'll meet you at Eleanor and Dale's suite."

"Alright, I'll see you there."

Ben and I part ways.

I hurry to my room, trying to appear calm, greeting and smiling at passengers as I pass through the massive ship, as if I wasn't just with a dead body.

Once I reach my room, I set the evidence box aside, ensuring to tuck it inside the closet and cover it with unused bedding in case someone tries to tamper with the case.

You can never be too careful in investigations.

After securing the evidence, I head back to the suites, only to find Ben pacing in front of Eleanor and Dale's room.

"Ben," I call out. "Is everything okay?"

Ben looks up, his bottom lip pinched between his teeth, a sign of his nerves. "Um, no. I don't think Dale is inside. No one's answering."

"Great," I mutter to myself, considering the fastest way to find Dale.

I could announce it on the ship, but I don't want to raise suspicions. I pull my radio from my pocket. "I'll call for aid without disclosing the... details."

"Good idea," Ben agrees.

I activate my radio and press the talk button. "Security team, this is Rose. We need support in locating Dale Bridges on the ship. I repeat, we need to locate Dale Bridges immediately. Thank you."

Thankfully, we all have a comprehensive list of passengers, so security can identify Dale from his submitted ID card.

"Noted, Miss Dela Cruz," someone from security responds.

Turning to Ben, I see the frustration etched on his features. He is the ship's captain, and someone just died under his watch.

For the second time now.

I try to console him. "Hey, Ben, you should probably sit tight for now. I can talk to Dale."

Ben shakes his head. "No, I'd rather be with you when we speak to him. This is terrible news to receive."

"Well, okay. But tell me if you need to step aside, alright?"

"Don't worry about me, Rose. But... thanks."

"Of course." I even rub his arm briefly. "Should we go see Allison? Maybe she's still with Dale."

"Alright. Her room's in the lower suites."

"Lead the way, Captain."

I follow Ben to the lower suites, watching him count the room numbers until he finally stops at room 1407.

Ben knocks on the door.

After a few seconds of shuffling, Allison's voice calls out from the other side, "

Coming!"

We hear more rustling before the door opens.

Allison, her hair a tangled mess and wearing a robe, peers through the slightly ajar door. "Ben, Rose, what a surprise! Is there anything I can do for you?"

Ben answers on our behalf. "Um, yeah, Rose mentioned she saw you leave the dining hall with Mr. Dale Bridges. We were wondering if he's here with you."

Allison blinks at us, a look of confusion crossing her face. She opens the door wider to let us in.

Her suite is a bit chaotic; half of her duvet is hanging off the bed, and several articles of clothing are strewn about the floor.

Allison chuckles sheepishly when she notices me looking around. "Sorry about the mess. I'm not exactly... tidy. But as you can see, Dale isn't here."

I seize the moment to ask, "Do you know where he is?"

"Um, no. After a quick chat at the dining hall, we just walked around the deck, then called it a night."

Ben suppresses a sigh, the frustration evident in his expression. "Well, alright. If you hear from him tonight, can you let me know?"

Allison's eyebrows rise in suspicion. "Y-yeah, sure. But... is everything okay?"

"Yeah, yeah," Ben tries to maintain a casual tone.

"Well, okay. I'll let you know if he reaches out," Allison assures us. "I'm sure he's just somewhere on the ship."

"I bet he is," Ben nods. "Well, good night."

"Good night, you two. Take it easy."

As we walk away from Allison's door, I can feel the tension rising. First, a dead body, and now a potentially missing person. But I try to stay optimistic—maybe Dale is just walking around the ship.

Once we're back in the corridor, I turn to my radio again. "Security, is there any update on locating Dale Bridges?"

Two seconds later, a reply comes in. "Nothing yet, Miss Dela Cruz. We're still looking."

"Okay, thanks," I respond, trying to mask my rising anxiety.

Ben, who has been listening closely to the radio transmissions, finally shows signs of stress. "I don't feel good about this, Rose. What do you say we unlock their suite?"

I'm still unfamiliar with the ship's protocols, but if it's the captain's advice, I trust him. "I think we should. Just to make sure Dale is... okay."

"Okay, let's go then."

Ben and I return to Eleanor and Dale's suite.

Standing outside the door, Ben produces the key card from his pocket and holds it up to the sensor.

As he places the card in front of the reader, the tiny light shifts from red to green, followed by a soft beep.

With that, Ben pushes the door open.

I hold my breath.

The lights in the threshold flicker on as Ben and I step into the empty suite.

Without wasting any time, Ben swiftly checks the bedroom and bathroom before returning to the living space, where the vast window overlooks... nothing.

It's too dark to see anything in the ocean.

Ben states the obvious. "Dale's not here."

This time, I let out a distressed sigh. "Well, it's a gigantic ship. He has to be somewhere, right? It's not like he can just jump overboard."

Ben flinches at my words. "He's here; we just have to find him."

But where? That's the question racing through my mind. And why did he suddenly... disappear?

This isn't how I envisioned my first night on the Midnight Tide.

Chapter 6

I sit up from the bed after hours of tossing and turning—this won't do.

I can't sleep at all.

The vivid image of Eleanor Bridges is etched behind my eyelids like the poster of my favorite singer plastered on my wall when I was fourteen.

The way her head tilted unnaturally. The now-permanent scowl on her face. Her rigid body beneath that silk blouse. Remembering all these details tells me I won't be sleeping for the next few days.

With a heavy sigh, Rex looks up from his bed in the corner, his eyes full of understanding. I inform him as if he can comprehend me, "I can't sleep, Rex. Want to go for an early walk with me, bud?"

Maybe he does understand me because he sits up and stretches his front paws, letting out a big yawn. I'll take that as a yes.

I quickly brush my teeth, wash my face, and throw on a knitted sweatshirt and some comfortable pants while I still can.

In just two and a half hours, my duty as the cruise director starts all over again—as if it even stopped earlier this evening.

Still, lightweight sneakers are far more comfortable than my pumps.

Unlike most dogs, Rex isn't excited about leashes, which is why I never got him one after he rejected the first four I bought him.

It took me a while to realize that Rex would follow me anywhere anyway.

That's exactly what he does now, walking alongside me as we navigate the ship's corridors.

Thankfully, Ben gave me a map of the ship, so I just need to head to the lower deck to find the morgue.

I know it's early, but I need to know what happened to Eleanor.

Foul play or not, I need to find out.

Of course, I end up lost while trying to find the morgue with a paper map. When I finally reach it, the locked door suggests it's still closed.

I sigh, turning back toward the upper deck.

However, when I glance over my shoulder, I realize Rex is no longer beside me. For a moment, panic rises in my chest, but then I remind myself that it's just how Rex is.

He'll show up.

It's still an hour before the breakfast buffet starts, but the kitchen staff is already bustling, preparing everything.

As I peek into the kitchen, my gaze drifts toward the dining hall entrance.

It's not like Eleanor's body is still there, but the thought makes me stop in my tracks.

Pushing open the enormous double doors, I find the servers fixing the tables and placing utensils in a neat, symmetrical line.

Near the windows, someone has cleaned Eleanor's table from last night.

My feet take me back there, searching the surroundings one last time in case I missed anything.

But I can tell there's been a replacement for the table-cloth, and someone has mopped the floor.

Unknown to the person who cleaned it, someone just died here.

Seeing Eleanor's empty seat churns my stomach. I call over a server. "Excuse me?"

The nearest attendant turns and jogs in my direction. "Good morning, Miss Dela Cruz. Can I help you?"

"Yes," I offer him a small smile. "I was wondering if we could have this seat removed."

The attendant looks at me, eyebrows furrowed. "It's... upon a passenger's request?"

I nod. "Yes, that's right."

He slowly agrees, "No problem, Miss Dela Cruz."

"Thank you."

I step aside as the server carries the upholstered chair out of the dining hall.

It's the only tangible action I can take to make Eleanor's death feel less... present in the dining hall. 499 other passengers will dine here, unaware that one has passed away right on this deck.

"Early morning, huh?" A voice calls from behind me.

I turn around to see Ben approaching in casual clothing, his hands tucked into his pockets. I respond, "Sleep eluded me."

"Same here," Ben exhales, noticing the empty seat at the table beside us. "You took care of that already, I see."

"I hope you don't mind. I just don't think anyone should... occupy the same seat."

"Don't worry about it. I was planning to do the same."

Seeing Ben here, I ask, "Oh, by the way, have we found Dale?"

Ben shakes his head. "I haven't spoken to security yet. I'll call Cole—"

"Oh no," I stop him, realizing it's still early. "Let Cole rest. I'm sure he's processing last night's events."

Ben nods. "I suppose one of us should get some sleep, huh?"

"Yeah, at least one of us."

Ben and I stand beside each other in complete silence, either sleep-deprived or disturbed by Eleanor's sudden death.

Then Ben's phone buzzes inside his pocket.

I watch him pull out his phone, his eyes widening at the sight of the caller ID. He quickly answers, "Dr. Bates, good morning."

Dr. Bates?

Now, that's the person I've been meaning to see for the last few hours. I can't help but move closer to Ben to hear their conversation.

But it's hard to listen over the clattering of cutlery, the sound of the sea, and the ship's humming engine. I only catch snippets of Ben's side. "Of course, Dr. Bates. We'll be there shortly."

The brief phone call ends quickly.

Ben looks at me, urgency in his eyes. "Dr. Bates wants us at the morgue now; he says he has the blood test results for Eleanor."

Finally.

"Let's go, then," I reply, stepping out of the dining hall.

On our way to the morgue, Ben sends Cole a message, informing him to join us if he's able.

Within five minutes, we arrive at the morgue. Dr. Bates is putting on his white coat, acknowledging our arrival. "Great, you're both here."

Ben responds, trying to catch his breath from our quick walk. "Thanks for the prompt action, Dr. Bates."

"Oh, don't mention it." Dr. Bates strides to his desk, retrieving a clipboard. "I'm just doing my job, considering the ship's morgue rarely gets... customers."

Quite the dark humor, I must say.

Dr. Bates rejoins us in the middle of the room, where the metal table is and where Eleanor lies, covered with a thin blanket.

Dr. Bates pulls the cover down slightly, revealing Eleanor's collarbone.

She looks... dead. Blue lips and ashen skin.

Dr. Bates looks at us. "Shall we begin?"

Ben nods. "Yes, we'll fill in the head of security later."

"Okay then," Dr. Bates puts on his glasses, sliding them down the bridge of his nose. "Well, I did the autopsy and ran whatever tests I could; I understand we're still a day away from port. My initial assumption was correct: Eleanor Bridges died from a heart attack. I note that there was a blockage in her coronary arteries, resulting in cardiac arrest."

Heart attack—just as I guessed.

"But that's the thing," Dr. Bates pauses, as if bracing himself to share something significant. "For her age, she seemed to have had a healthy heart before this. So, I decided to run some blood tests, and I found something quite interesting."

Ben and I exchange curious glances. "What is it, doctor?" Ben asks.

"I saw something in her blood under the microscope. Since I don't have all the right equipment here, I sent a photo to a colleague, and she just got back to me this morning."

I want to scold Dr. Bates for pausing so much—I need to know what he found.

Finally, he continues, "I discovered maitotoxin in Eleanor's blood."

Maitotoxin? What the hell is that? If it weren't for the word 'toxin,' I'd be completely clueless. So, it must be some kind of... poison, right?

Does this mean she's been poisoned?

While Ben processes this information, I blurt out, "Maitotoxin? Is it some kind of poison?"

"To be frank, I didn't know it myself," Dr. Bates admits. "But my colleague does. Maitotoxin is indeed poisonous. You can get it from eating contaminated shellfish. This toxin is quick—causing heart failure almost immediately."

I can feel the blood drain from my face. "Shellfish?"

Ben mutters to himself, loud enough for us to hear, "We served clams at last night's dinner."

Panic rises within me.

Does that mean others could have been poisoned?

I quickly turn to Ben. "Captain, did anyone report to the clinic about food poisoning from last night?"

Ben retrieves his phone, scrolling through messages. "I'm not sure. But I haven't received any alerts from the clinic, especially regarding mass poisoning."

Before I can respond, we hear fast footsteps approaching the hallway.

Turning around, Cole arrives, leaning against the door-frame as he catches his breath. "I came as soon as I received your message, Captain. What did I miss?"

Ben looks at me, urging me to break the news to Cole. I take a deep breath and say, "Eleanor died from a heart attack."

Cole swallows hard, his voice trembling. "Does she have a cardiovascular disease?"

"Not exactly."

"Then what?"

I almost can't bring myself to say it, but Cole's wide, expectant eyes compel me. "She's been... poisoned."

Chapter 7

For a moment, I think Cole hasn't heard me—he merely blinks at us, shock etched on his face, before saying nothing.

Then, two seconds later, his knees buckle, and he nearly loses his balance. He would have fallen if he hadn't clung to the doorframe.

"Cole!" Ben reacts immediately, stepping closer. "Are you okay?"

Cole regains his footing, shaking his head as if trying to clear the fog. "Sorry. It's just that... in my years as a security officer on a cargo ship, I've never dealt with... murder."

Murder—what a dreadful word. Just hearing it makes my skin crawl.

Upon hearing that term, I turn to look at Dr. Bates, who swiftly responds matter-of-factly, "Let's not use the word 'murder' for now. Maitotoxin is only ingested from contaminated shellfish. Perhaps Mrs. Bridges simply had bad luck and ate a clam that was unfortunately tainted."

Though Cole is the head of security, he looks so innocent with his troubled expression, as if he might throw up from seasickness.

"But the rest of the passengers had clams for dinner too, didn't they? What if..."

His words trail off, but judging by his expression, I know what he's trying to say.

What if more passengers were poisoned?

"Oh God," I can't help but exclaim. "I hope not."

Before our anxiety can spiral, Ben interjects, "Okay. I think now is the best time for all of us to calm down. We need to be rational about this. If this maitotoxin immediately causes heart failure, we'd have more dead bodies on our hands since last night."

Ben's voice is therapeutic—steadying. He makes a valid point.

He continues, "After dinner last night, we only saw Eleanor. She may just be the unlucky one. But we can't let our guard down. We need to investigate this quietly."

Cole and I nod in agreement.

I can see Ben's mechanical brain whirring into action. "First things first, I'll sit down with the head chef to discuss quality control of the ingredients. Cole, I need you to discreetly interview the passengers. Find out if anyone else got sick."

Cole's demeanor shifts from nervous to motivated.

Then Ben turns to me. "And Rose, I need you to find Dale. He needs to know about this as soon as possible. For all we know, he and Eleanor might have shared a plate."

I nod firmly. "Okay. I'll find him. No matter what."

With our distinct missions laid out, we disperse from the morgue.

My task seems far simpler than interviewing 499 passengers, so I opt for the most logical step first: looking for Dale in their suite.

It's only a few minutes after seven in the morning, so the chances of him still sleeping are high. But still, it's odd.

If he's in his suite, why isn't he looking for his grandmother?

I make my way to the upper decks to visit Eleanor and Dale's suite once more.

I knock on the door lightly at first, but after a minute, I knock with more purpose—a bit more aggressive than I prefer.

And still, nothing.

Now I'm genuinely worried. What if Dale really did share a plate with his grandmother and is dead somewhere on the ship?

What if he fell overboard during a heart attack?

Snap out of it, Rose. I remind myself this isn't the time to let poisonous thoughts win. We have enough poison on this ship already—one, and it's called maitotoxin.

And it should have been zero.

For now, I take a deep breath to think clearly.

I could spend hours scouring the ship blindly looking for Dale, and it still probably won't be enough.

I need an alternative way to track him.

As that thought crosses my mind, I glance at the upper right corner of the hallway. Hoisted up on the wall is a security camera.

That's right! I can trace Dale's movements from last night through the cameras.

Security cameras surround the ship; I should have thought of this last night!

I quickly head to the security office, where the camera feeds are monitored in real time.

The security personnel on duty greet me, and I return the gesture.

I head straight to the backroom where the 'action' is taking place.

Behind the door are massive screens displaying multiple camera feeds. And 'multiple' is an understatement—at least a hundred boxes of moving images fill the room, each labeled with room names and numbers.

A security officer swivels in his chair, and I call for his attention.

"Hi, excuse me," I say.

The young man looks up from his cup of coffee, already lively from what must be his first cup. "Miss Dela Cruz—ma'am, we weren't expecting you here. Are you looking for Mr. Hester?"

"Oh, no," I reply. "I was just with him earlier. I'm here to ask if I could access the security footage from last night."

"From last night? Sure," he replies, standing up and awkwardly bumping his hip against the table in the cramped room. "Have a seat, ma'am."

I slide into the chair. "Alright, thank you."

He leans over next to me, navigating the system with the mouse. "What room are we looking at today?"

"The dining hall. Sometime around 9:30 to 10:00 last night," I say.

"Okay. Let me just pull that up for you."

I watch as he types and clicks for a moment, then a larger tab pops up on the screen, showing a high-resolution video of the dining hall from last night. This camera view is from a high vantage point.

From this distance, I can make out a few familiar faces, including Dale and Allison, standing in the corner, a few tables away from Eleanor, who is... clutching her chest.

My heart sinks at the sight.

From this angle, it looks like she's just suffering from heartburn.

Slowly, she stops holding onto the front of her blouse, losing consciousness as her head tilts lower onto the table.

Like she simply fell asleep.

"What are we looking for, ma'am?" the guy beside me asks, pulling me back to reality.

I swallow the sudden lump in my throat.

Looking at the part where Dale and Allison are still chatting and laughing, I point to their images. "I need you to track their movements around the ship; see where they went, especially that guy."

"Okay, ma'am," he agrees, speeding up the video until they leave the dining hall.

He switches to another camera, this time following Dale and Allison down the dining hall hallway.

Just as Allison said, they head onto the deck, where they walk around, deep in conversation.

Somewhere in the fifth frame, they vanish into the crowd by the poolside bar—also known as the Solstice Bar.

"Where'd they go?" I mutter, frustration creeping in.

The guy rewinds the footage to the last moment we could still see them before they were lost in the crowd of people enjoying the night.

He does that three times before saying, "Um, let me try all the routes leading out from this point. Just give me a second..."

I thought this would be easier, but tracking two people across a hundred frames is proving difficult.

As I wait, we suddenly hear a commotion from outside the backroom; some officers are half-shouting, sending someone—or something—away.

I stand from my chair, heading out of the room. "What's happening—"

Following the two officers chasing something across the floor, I spot my brown and black beagle running around, only stopping when he sees me.

"Rex!" I call, relieved to see him. He races to my feet.

Turning to the officers, I explain, "It's alright. It's my dog; he must've been looking for me."

I crouch down to scratch Rex's chin, but he seems anxious.

Rex stands on his hind legs, tapping my knee, but I tell him, "Now's not the time to play, Rex. I'm busy."

He circles back to me, then turns his whole body toward the exit, his nose pointing in that direction.

If Rex weren't such a special dog, I might brush off his invitation. But he's special—he's helped me solve a case before. So, I stand up and turn to the backroom. "Keep following them. I'll be right back."

With that, I let my dog lead the way.

I just hope it's worth my time.

Though Rex is special, he's still a dog. Once, he led me out to the backyard to watch him chase squirrels. Another time, he interrupted my breakfast just to bark at the mailman.

But today is different.

Rex runs ahead of me with determination and certainty, making precise turns as we navigate the ship.

We climb four flights of stairs before arriving at the lower suites—the same deck Ben and I visited last night.

Rex darts down the hallway, prompting me to jog to keep up.

Then he halts and sits in front of a specific door: Room 1407.

Allison's suite.

What?

I approach Rex, whispering, "What is it, boy?"

Rex barks once at the door before looking up at me, as if urging me to knock.

I have no idea why—I'm unsure if Allison has another dog onboard, and Rex wants to play. Or if it's something entirely different.

But I know there's only one way to find out: to knock.

I face the door to Allison's suite and raise my arm at an angle to knock.

As I push my closed hand forward, the door swings open.

While I expect to see Allison on the other side, it's a different person who greets me. His hair is a bit of a bird's nest, and his shirt is wrinkled, as if he just rolled out of bed.

Staring at each other in surprise, I say, "Mr. Dale Bridges? What are you doing here?"

Dale rubs the sleep from his eyes, clearly caught off guard. "Rose? I... um, I didn't expect to see you so early."

I study him closely, noting the disheveled look and the way he fidgets with the hem of his shirt. "Mr. Bridges... I need to discuss something with you."

Chapter 8

Before we head inside, Dale halts in front of his suite, completely unaware of what I'm about to reveal. "Did my grandmother ask you to look for me?"

My chest tightens at how nonchalant he sounds.

He continues, "Because if she did, she's way out of line. I'm an adult, and I can sleep wherever I please."

It's none of my business if Dale and Allison spent the night together. It only matters if this is a murder—and for now, it isn't.

"No, your grandmother didn't ask me to find you," I reply, though I know she couldn't, even if she wanted to.

Dale squints at me, confusion flickering in his eyes. " Okay... then why are you walking me back to my suite again?"

"There's something I need to tell you, Mr. Bridges."

"Can you tell me now?"

I glance around the hallway, where anyone could be lurking. Anyone with ears could overhear the unfortunate news I'm about to deliver.

"I was hoping we could talk about it in private," I insist.

"Well, okay then," Dale finally pulls out his key card and taps it against the door.

He opens it, and Rex and I follow him inside.

Once Dale shuts the door, Rex stations himself by the entrance, ever the vigilant protector.

Dale watches Rex, a smile creeping across his face. "Is he some sort of guard dog?"

I glance at Rex. "You could say that. He loves looking after me."

"How adorable." Dale leans back against the couch, spreading his arms over the backrest. "Is my grandma here?"

"N-no," I stammer, choking on my words.

"I knew it. She's with Captain Anderson again, isn't she? My grandma completely adores him. Sometimes I think she wishes Captain Anderson was her grandson."

Dale's light chuckle sends a pang through my chest.

I hate being the one to deliver this bad news.

Dale Bridges is carefree, with the world at his feet, a privilege partly granted by his grandmother... who is gone now.

I can't even muster a smile at his joke, leaving Dale awkwardly shifting in his seat. He clears his throat. "Anyway, what were you going to tell me, Miss Dela Cruz? Or can I just call you Rose?"

"Rose is fine, Mr. Bridges—"

"Dale. Just call me Dale."

"Alright, Dale," I start, but I pause, gathering my thoughts. "I realize there's no easy way to say this, so I'll just get on with it."

Dale's eyes are on me, anticipation swirling in their depths, blissfully unaware of the heartbreak that's about to hit him.

"Your grandmother... had a heart attack last night."

Dale's face barely registers the words. He scratches his eyebrow, disbelief etched across his features. "A heart attack? That's impossible. For her age, Grandma has a healthy heart. She does full physical check-ups every four months."

Except Eleanor's heart attack isn't health-related.

She lived healthily enough to meet an accidental death—assuming it was an accident.

But Dale is in denial; I can see it. Years of studying human behavior help me recognize the signs.

Is it denial, or is he putting on an act?

In that moment, I decide it's best not to tell him how Eleanor died—not yet.

Until I'm sure this isn't a murder, Dale is a potential suspect. So, I simply tell him what he needs to hear. "Dale, I'm sorry. But your grandmother had a heart attack last night, and she—she died."

His expression goes blank.

Dale stares at me, as if I've just recited a dull grocery list.

But as I study him closer, I realize he isn't really seeing me—he's detaching.

Those words are hard to absorb, and his brain is refusing to process them. A defense mechanism.

"Dale, did you hear me?" I prompt gently.

His gaze remains distant, like reality is dawning on him at lightning speed.

Worried he'll break, I reach out, touching his knee lightly. "Dale?"

He flinches at my touch, finally finding his voice. "N-no, no. Uh... I heard you. I just—wow. What do I say?"

"Take your time," I assure him. "I'm just here."

Dale runs a hand over his face, pressing hard against his mouth as if to hold everything together.

I watch him frantically, yet calmly, cycle through his emotions—biting his hands, shaking them, opening and closing them, before finally resting them in his lap. "God-dammit. So, she's... gone?"

I keep waiting for Dale to cry, but I remind myself that grief doesn't always manifest outwardly.

I nod. "Yes. I'm so sorry for your loss."

He buries his face in his hands. "It's my fault, isn't it? I—I made her wait all night, and she was probably worried about me. I—I made her too anxious, didn't I?"

I know his questions are rhetorical, so I let him continue.

"I should've known something was wrong when she didn't call me at least an hour after I left her at dinner last night. I should've known something happened when I turned on my phone this morning, and it didn't explode with messages and calls from grandma. Fuck me."

The curse words are forgivable, if not unavoidable.

Grief is unique to everyone.

So, I sit quietly in the chair, listening to Dale's ragged breaths as he tries to find some semblance of calm. When he finally looks up at the ceiling, I say, "You know it's not your fault, right? Things happen. Some things are inevitable. Don't punish yourself for them."

I doubt he's in the right headspace to absorb my advice, but he nods out of politeness. "So, where is she? My grand-ma?"

"She's at the morgue."

"Can I see her?"

"Of course."

I lead him down to the morgue, where Dr. Bates has placed Eleanor's body in the mortuary cabinet to preserve it.

As we approach the morgue, Dale halts outside the door. "Is she... really dead?"

Once again, his denial rears its head. I wouldn't have brought him here if Eleanor weren't dead, but I understand his pain.

"Dale, you don't have to look at her now if you can't."

"But I have to be sure because I don't get it. How can it happen overnight?"

I want to say, through a contaminated shellfish, but I reply instead, "I know there's nothing I can say to make you feel better, but for what it's worth, your grandmother wouldn't want you to blame yourself."

"What do I even tell my family? They all think grandma is just enjoying her time."

I wish I had the right answer to that. "I don't know. But I'm sure they won't blame you, either."

"It's a canon event, huh?"

"All deaths are."

Dale stares at the morgue door, his gaze fierce enough to bore a hole through it. Then he takes a deep breath. "Okay, I think I'm ready. If I don't do it now, I won't be able to do it at all."

I nod, opening the morgue door before he changes his mind.

Dr. Bates looks up from his chart as I announce, "Eleanor Bridges' grandson is here."

Dr. Bates glances over my shoulder at Dale, who stands hunched and heavy with grief. "I'm so sorry for your loss, son," he says gently.

Dale nods, his voice barely a whisper. "Thank you."

We follow Dr. Bates to the corner of the room, where the mortuary cabinet stands. He opens the center cabinet in the middle row and pulls out the metal tray.

I can't help but watch Dale as he looks at the white blanket covering his grandmother's body.

Just as Dr. Bates reaches for the cover over Eleanor's head, Dale stops him. "Wait. I—I'll do it myself."

Dale is shaking now, trembling under the weight of reality. He turns to us, his voice breaking. "Can I have a few moments with her, please?"

"Of course," Dr. Bates replies, walking with me out of the morgue.

As we close the door behind us, I peer through the small glass pane, watching as Dale lifts the cover. His back begins to heave as he finally lets out a heart-wrenching cry.

Dr. Bates sighs behind me. "Ironic, isn't it? He and his grandmother were supposed to be having fun on the Midnight Tide. Yet here he is, grieving."

Chapter 9

"God, I've been looking for you everywhere!" After running around all morning, Stacy finally spots me on one of the upper decks.

It's nearly lunchtime now, and her expression is a mixture of worry and frustration. "I didn't know where you were! You're not answering your phone, and I couldn't even find Captain Anderson. I thought you eloped!"

"Stace," I say, letting my voice drag as I keep walking, allowing her to trail behind me for now. "It's just been a busy morning, that's all."

"How busy?" she asks, her tone suggesting disbelief—or maybe just curiosity.

With Stacy, I know it's best to come clean. While we've agreed to keep a tight lid on Eleanor's death, Stacy is an exception. She's someone I trust with my life.

I sigh, my wide eyes and raised eyebrows giving away that something is indeed up. "Very busy."

Stacy gasps quietly. "Oh no. What happened?"

I keep moving until we reach the terrace, where the salty air hits our faces, and the sound of the ocean splashing provides a bit of privacy.

I pull Stacy aside, scanning the area to ensure we're out of earshot. "There's been a...death on the ship."

"What?" she exclaims, struggling to keep her voice down. "Who was it? What happened?"

"Eleanor Bridges."

"Of Emerald Hotels?"

"You know her?"

"Well, yeah! She's notorious in the hotel industry," Stacy says, scrunching her nose in disbelief. "The real deal in European real estate. What happened to her?"

I dread saying it out loud; it feels wrong to share such grim news, even with my sister. "She's been food poisoned."

"Oh my god." Stacy's eyes light up as if she's had an epiphany. "Is that why security officers were doing 'food surveys' this morning? I found it odd. I mean, by this morning, we'd only had three meals on board, and surveys usually don't happen until the last few days."

Smart. That must be how Cole is collecting feedback about last night's meal.

I can hardly focus on anything else.

I even had to escort Dale back to his room to make sure he was okay. I need to check on him for lunch—he already skipped breakfast, not even a drop of coffee.

"Glad you're okay, though," I tell Stacy, who shrugs.

"Yeah, but how unfortunate. Did more people...die?"

I shake my head quickly. "No, thank God. At least, I don't think so. I didn't hear about any other passengers getting sick."

"Good, good." Stacy seems confused, even if she feigns relief. "But why was it just Eleanor?"

Murder—I almost say it out loud.

Instead, I reply, "Contaminated shellfish. That's our speculation for now; we don't know for sure if it's just her. We haven't figured out whether it was intentional."

"And if it is?" Stacy presses.

I open my mouth to answer, then close it again.

What can I even say to that? It's one thing to have a death on board, but murder?

So, I whisper my wishful thinking into the breeze—or rather, to Stacy. "I hope not."

I tap her arm so we can keep walking. "But even if it isn't, it would definitely put Captain Anderson in a tough spot. Call it negligence or manslaughter or homicide—whatever Eleanor Bridges' lawyers can conjure up. It's the captain who would have to face them. He's in charge."

What a dreadful thought.

I can only imagine how stressed Ben is about all of this. As if having a renowned archaeologist die on board wasn't enough.

And now a billionaire?

What is this, a cursed cruise ship?

I shake off the dark thoughts, my phone pinging with a new message.

It's from Ben: Meet me at the bridge. Cole is here.

I glance at Stacy, raising my phone. "Speak of the devil. The captain calls."

"Can I come?" Stacy asks. While I appreciate her enthusiasm, it might be better to keep her out of this for now. This could still be an accident.

"It's official business for now, Stace. Plus, it's almost lunchtime. You should head to the dining hall."

She pouts at me. "You want me to eat after telling me that one of our passengers has been food poisoned?"

Thankfully, no one is close enough to hear her say that.

I'm already walking away as I respond. "Just...avoid the shellfish for now!"

"Thanks for the advice!" Stacy calls after me, laced with sarcasm.

I jog in my two-inch block heels as I ascend the cruise ship toward the bridge—the ship's command center.

Ben's fortress.

It's my first time in a ship's bridge. The U-shaped room sits at the top of the vessel, with windows all around, offering panoramic views unobstructed by the ship's structure.

Buttons, monitors, tables, and chairs clutter the space, looking like something out of a sci-fi film.

Nine people occupy the room—Ben and Cole included. Both are standing by a small conference table, and neither looks pleased.

I announce my presence. "Captain, I'm here."

"Rose," Ben replies, glancing up. "Come here and join us."

I walk over to the table, taking a seat alongside the two of them.

Turning to the stack of papers in the center of the table, I ask Cole, "How's the survey?"

"Great," he says, but his expression doesn't match his words. "I was just telling the Captain how last night's dinner was amazing."

"So, no complaints?"

"None whatsoever."

Ben adds, "Our only complaint was that the minestrone was too salty. That's it."

The horror sinks in, heavy on my shoulders. "So, it's just Eleanor?"

Ben nods. "I also spoke with the head chef about the ingredients. We've been sourcing our seafood from the same supplier for the last five years; not once has an incident like this occurred. The chances they made such a deadly mistake are slim."

I already know where this conversation is heading, but I don't want to say it. "So, what are we trying to say?"

Cole and Ben exchange glances.

After a few tense seconds, Ben finally says, "Considering everything, there's a high probability it's...murder."

I can't hide my disappointment; even my sigh feels like a weight in my chest.

Ben looks at me expectantly. "So, Miss Private Investigator, what's our move now?"

In moments like this, pride in my profession feels misplaced. While solving murders is part of the job—the better part—I'd rather follow cheating spouses any day than profit from someone's death.

Thankfully, Ben isn't paying me to solve murders. I put on my detective hat over my cruise director's cap. "We find the killer, starting with the suspects."

Cole, who's been deep in thought, pipes up. "It makes sense that Dale Bridges is a suspect, right? I mean, he disappeared after his grandmother died."

Even witnessing Dale's grief, I have to agree with Cole. I remind myself to remain rational; emotions can't cloud judgment. "I also found him in Allison's suite this morning."

Ben's brow furrows in confusion. "What do you mean? We went there last night."

"I know," I take a deep breath. "But maybe he returned in the evening? Perhaps Allison hid him?"

"Why would Allison hide him?"

"I don't know, either. I'm just thinking out loud."

Cole taps his pen against the blank paper in front of him. "That situation itself is suspicious enough. So, Dale Bridges is suspect number one. Who else?"

I pause, recalling every passenger Eleanor could have crossed paths with. I turn to Ben, my alarm growing. "Oh! What about that attendant Eleanor humiliated yesterday over a glass of water? She was understandably upset."

Ben remembers this too. "Y-yeah, it makes sense if she's angry…"

Cole looks at us innocently. "Is this attendant angry enough to kill Eleanor?"

Since I was the one who intervened, I can answer. "She was upset to the point of tears. But would she kill Eleanor? We can't really know. Some murderers have lesser motives than being humiliated in public."

Cole scribbles on his paper. "Do we have a name?"

"No," I confess, realizing I didn't think it was necessary. "I didn't get her name."

Ben reassures us. "I remember her face. I can pull up all the employee files, and we can look through them."

"Okay," I nod, pausing to consider. "Would she have access to the kitchen? We're looking for someone who could have tampered with Eleanor's dinner."

Ben ponders this. "The kitchen staff and the servers both have access. The girl began her shift at 8:00 this morning. Yesterday, she couldn't have worked more than eight hours."

"But could her shift have stopped her from entering the kitchen?"

"Well, there's no protocol about it…"

"So, no?"

"N-no."

I nod at Cole, who diligently takes down notes, as if documenting meeting minutes. He asks, "So, Dale and the attendant?"

In the back of my mind, I don't think a server could just waltz into the kitchen and tamper with food, especially someone from the morning shift. I respond, "And someone from the kitchen. So it's Dale, the attendant, and the kitchen staff."

Chapter 10

Dale opens the door to his suite, his eyes swollen, lips chapped, and skin as pale as ash. He barely glances at us. "What is it?"

It breaks my heart to do this to Dale—to interview him about his grandmother's murder.

Just a few hours ago, he was crying by her corpse, and now he's a suspect in her death.

What a cruel twist life can deliver.

Cole looks at me, expecting me to take the lead since Dale seems more familiar with me. So, I say, "Can we come in, Dale? We need to talk to you."

Dale studies us, hesitation flickering across his features. Then he pushes the door open wider. "I've already heard the worst news today, so I may as well."

I step inside, with Cole following closely.

Dale shuts the door behind us, sealing off the world outside.

He wraps a blanket tightly around his shoulders as he sinks onto the couch, devoid of the energy to invite us to sit. "So, what now?"

Cole and I take a seat on the opposite couch.

I begin, "Dale, I know today has been unimaginable for you. On behalf of the Midnight Tide, I'm truly sorry for your loss."

The easygoing guy I met yesterday feels like a distant memory. He's drained and irritable. "I'm sure you didn't come here just to offer your condolences again."

I bite my inner cheek, forcing myself to navigate this difficult conversation.

Cole nods at me, unsure how to broach the topic himself.

I realize it's all on me now. "You're right, Dale. We're not here for that. We've been looking into your grandmother's death, and we have reason to suspect that there's been...foul play."

I still can't bring myself to say murder out loud; it feels too surreal.

Dale blinks at me, confusion clouding his features. "Foul play? You mean, she's been...murdered?"

I slowly nod. "Considering the circumstances—"

"What circumstances?" he interrupts. "You said she died of a heart attack. Now someone has murdered her? What? Someone induced her heart attack?"

"Like you said, Mrs. Eleanor Bridges had a healthy heart. As it turns out, we found poison in her bloodstream."

Dale scoffs, throwing his hands up in frustration. "Great! So not only do I have to tell my family that grandma is dead, but also that someone murdered her. Just...great."

I recognize that his emotions are spiraling right now. So, I try to be patient.

I wait a moment before continuing. "Before anything else, Dale, we need some information. It's...procedural."

This time, I give Cole a nudge. He clears his throat. "Mr. Bridges, where did you go shortly after leaving the dining hall last night?"

Dale's brows knit together at the question. He drops the blanket off his shoulders and leans back on the couch, scowling. "Ah, I see. You think I killed my grandmother?"

Cole quickly adds, "Like Miss Dela Cruz said, it's only procedural. We just need to clear your name for the police report."

Nice save.

If Dale doesn't buy it, he doesn't show it.

Instead, he shakes his head but still responds. "I was at the pool bar with another passenger. Her name's Allison Rye."

Dale raises an eyebrow at me. "You found me in her suite this morning."

Now is the perfect time to probe him further. "Speaking of, we looked for you there last night, but Allison said you weren't in her suite. Did you...go somewhere else before heading back there?"

"Let me set one thing straight, 'detectives,'" Dale makes air quotes with his fingers. "It's none of your business how I spent my night. But since you're here to accuse me of murder, I'll tell you where I was last night."

He sounds like he'd throw punches if he could.

"I asked Allison not to tell you that I was in there because my grandmother has a knack for sticking her nose into everyone's business, including my relationships. So, I asked her not to say anything. Happy?"

I feel guilty putting him in this awkward position—but this guilt is what the real killer should feel.

Not wanting to prolong the conversation, I decide to cut it short. If Dale's telling the truth, we can easily verify it through the security cameras.

From the moment he entered Allison's room to when he left.

Noticing that Cole is about to speak up for more questions, I raise my voice to overshadow him. "Thank you for that, Mr. Bridges. That's all for now."

I can feel Cole's questioning gaze on me.

Still, I stand from my seat and gently pull on Cole's sleeve.

"Let's go, Cole. We should let Mr. Bridges rest."

Dale says nothing more; he just glares at us as we exit the suite.

Once the door closes behind us, Cole asks, "What was that about? We were just getting him to talk."

I shake my head. "It feels wrong to press him while he's in the depths of his grief; we have enough information, anyway."

"We do?"

"Yes. If Dale is lying, we'll find out. This ship has over a hundred security cameras. We can check if he really went to Allison's suite from the pool bar."

"Oh, you're right." Cole wriggles his nose. "I'm sorry. I didn't have any training for...solving murders."

"Neither do I," I admit. "I'm just winging it. No one can tell, right?"

Cole chuckles softly. "Yeah. In the meantime, I'll ask some of my officers to check the cameras in front of Allison's suite between the hours of 21:00 and 22:00 last night."

"Cool," I say with a small smile, then I turn to the copy of the resume Ben gave us earlier—the one for the girl Eleanor humiliated. "We should also talk to Susie Lowe."

While Cole relays orders to his security officers, I start tracking down Susie at one of the ship's bars.

On the Midnight Tide, there are three bars: the Solstice Bar, the poolside bar; the Sunset Bar, just below the bridge; and the Meridian Bar, which is inside the ship.

Cole and I head toward the Meridian Bar.

With its carpeted floors, oak furniture, and warm yellow lights, the Meridian Bar exudes a touch of Victorian architecture.

In the corner, I spot Susie Lowe serving chilled drinks to a few passengers.

We wait for her to return to the bar before approaching her. "Susie?"

She turns, eyes widening at the sight of me alongside the head of security. "Miss Dela Cruz...? Can I help you?"

I scan the room, then point to an empty table in the corner. "Can we talk to you over there?"

Susie looks nervous; the lines on her face betray her anxiety. "Um, okay..."

Before joining us, she serves us each a glass of water, which we gratefully accept.

Sitting across from us, she asks, "Am I in trouble? Did the old lady from yesterday complain about me?"

Her words almost immediately make me doubt our suspicions about her. She seems too innocent to have orchestrated a poisoning.

Rose, don't fool yourself. I remind myself.

So, I regain my composure. "No, she didn't, Susie. But we have a minor concern. We just need to ask you a few questions."

"Okay."

"Starting with...what time did your shift end yester-day?"

"Um, 4:00 p.m. Although I stayed an extra hour because they needed help at the Solstice Bar."

"Then where did you go after that?"

"Back to the crew cabin," she replies without hesitation, while Cole writes everything down.

I continue. "Do you mind telling us where you were between eight and ten in the evening?"

By now, Susie seems to sense my line of questioning. Still, she cooperates. "Um, we had dinner in the cafeteria at around eight. Then I showered before heading back to the cabin to rest for the night."

"So, cafeteria, shower area, and then the crew cabin?"

"That's right."

"You didn't go anywhere else during that time?"

Susie hesitates, likely understanding why we're asking. But she remains polite enough to answer. "If going to the restroom counts, then yes. I went to the restroom about three times during those hours."

We can verify everything she says through security cam-eras, but with her being this cooperative, we might not even need to.

So, I let her off easy. "Last question, Susie. Is there any-one who can vouch for you? Someone who can confirm you were in those places at those times?"

Susie nods, glancing around as if searching for someone. "That's Hail. She's my friend and roommate in the crew cabin. We share the same shift, so we do most things to-gether."

I point to a blonde-haired woman nearby. "Hail, you said?"

"Yes."

"Alright," I smile at Susie, hoping to ease her worries. "Thank you, Susie. You can return to work now."

With that, Cole and I approach Hail to ask her about Susie's whereabouts—and just as Susie said, they were together the entire time after Susie's shift at the Solstice Bar.

Fool-proof alibi.

Unless, of course, Hail is involved—something I'll keep in mind for a later conversation if necessary.

Meanwhile, a security officer radios Cole, reporting that Dale entered Allison's suite at exactly 9:53 p.m. last night.

So, Dale didn't lie—Allison did at his request.

Both of our suspects have alibis. But those alibis don't resolve one crucial question: how was Eleanor's meal poisoned?

I write Eleanor's name in bold on the whiteboard. Below it, arrows lead to 'Dale Bridges,' 'Susie Lowe,' and 'Kitchen Staff ???.'

Under their names, I list motives, means, and opportunities.

For Dale, I mark means and opportunity; he could easily bring poison when he boarded the ship, and he had dinner with his grandmother, giving him the chance to slip poison into her meal.

But what's his motive?

For Susie, I check motive and opportunity. While she likely couldn't bring poison onto the ship—security is strict for crew members—she has a motive. Eleanor humiliated her. As for opportunity, she could sneak into the kitchen just before dinner.

Finally, the unknown kitchen staff.

I check means and opportunity for that. Bringing in contaminated shellfish is easy for someone who works in the kitchen. It would be simple to serve it specifically to Eleanor.

But who is this person, and what vendetta do they have against Eleanor?

As I stare at the whiteboard Ben provided in one of the smaller conference rooms, I scratch my head for more useful information.

Dale and Susie have alibis, but they haven't completely cleared the motives, means, and opportunity test.

"Here are the documents you ordered," Cole's voice breaks the silence as he enters, carrying a hefty box filled with papers.

Roughly 700, to be precise.

With help from his security team, I'd requested background checks on all the passengers and crew members.

From there, I can find anyone with connections to Eleanor.

Connections and vendettas.

I move toward the heavy box. "Thanks, Cole."

His eyes are bloodshot, likely from staring at a computer screen for hours on end.

I tell him, "You don't have to stay up with me tonight. My sister will be helping me, anyway. She'll be here shortly."

Cole shakes his head firmly. "No, no. I want to be here. I want to help."

"Not if you're exhausted." I point to his crumpled uniform. "How about you take a nap and join us when you're re-energized?"

"But you haven't rested either."

"I wasn't the one checking backgrounds for the last nine hours. I'll be fine."

Stacy rushes into the conference room, catching our attention. "I'm here!"

The moment Cole sees my sister, his demeanor shifts.

Understandably, he finds Stacy beautiful—who could blame him?

"Stacy," I smile at her. "This is the ship's head of security, Cole Hester."

Stacy turns to Cole, extending her hand. "I'm Stacy Dela Cruz, Rose's sister."

Cole looks starstruck. "Um, h-hi."

"You'll be joining us tonight?"

"Y-yeah."

"What?" I exclaim. "Cole, you need to rest for a while. Remember?"

Cole snaps back to reality. "Oh, that's right."

He scurries out of the room, glancing back a few times before disappearing down the hall.

Stacy, either oblivious to her beauty or just used to it, takes a seat in one of the swiveling chairs. "Before we start, I came here with 'intel.'"

"Intel?" I raise an eyebrow at her.

"Valuable information!"

"I know what it means. So, what is it?"

Stacy slides her phone across the table toward me, explaining what I'm about to discover. "The Bridges are in the middle of an inheritance war. Apparently, Eleanor 'warned' her family she would cut everyone off from the will over a charity dinner gone wrong."

Hearing that, I turn back to the whiteboard.

The word 'motive' under Dale's name suddenly looks ominously like murder to me.

Chapter 11

It's only 6:00 a.m. when Cole calls—thankfully, I haven't slept yet, so answering his call is easy.

"Good morning, Cole," I say over a suppressed yawn. "Got anything for me?"

"Actually, yes," his voice is tense, no time for small talk. "I think it'd be best if you come down to the security office."

Glancing at Stacy, who's still asleep on my bed, I rise from my desk, momentarily leaving behind the scattered papers and my laptop, which has been running all night with tab after tab of searches.

I could use the walk. "I'll be there in five."

Quietly, I leave the room, trying not to wake Stacy, and make my way to the security office.

When I arrive, Cole is waiting for me in the back room, two cups of coffee steaming on the counter.

"I took the liberty of making you some coffee," Cole says. "I figured you had a long night."

I take one of the cups, grateful. "Thank you. As you can see from the bags under my eyes, I definitely need it."

"Well, have a seat. I'm going to show you something."

"Alright."

Cole stands next to me as he plays a security video clip from the night of Eleanor's murder; the camera is inside the kitchen.

Over twenty people are bustling around, busy with their tasks.

"What am I looking at?" I ask, narrowing my focus.

Cole pauses the video, pointing to a staff member near the doors. In front of them are two plates of the night's main dish—the one with the clams.

"Watch what they do next," he instructs.

I focus intently as they pull something out of their pocket.

The camera is positioned too high for me to see exactly what it is. Either way, the person's hand appears to place something on the plate before they exit the kitchen.

Cole stops the video and switches to another frame from a camera right outside the kitchen door.

The person has their head down as they carry a tray with two entrees down the dining hall, heading straight for Eleanor and Dale's table.

Cole changes the frame again, this time to a camera closer to Eleanor's table.

Whoever that server is, they seem to know their way around the ship and where the cameras are positioned.

Still keeping their head down, they serve the meal to Eleanor and Dale, who are too engrossed in an argument to notice who delivers the food.

We follow the same person through multiple frames until they finally exit the kitchen in a hurry, disappearing into the hallway, right where there's a blind spot.

Goddammit.

"Do you have any idea who that is?" Cole asks rhetorically.

"Can we zoom in?"

"We can, but I've been watching the same thing for more than an hour now, and there's never a moment when this person faces the camera."

Well, of course.

Despite my frustration, I refuse to let it get to me. "I guess it's safe to assume it's one of the kitchen staff."

"We could assume that," Cole agrees. "But that means we'll be interviewing at least fifty more people—on duty and off duty."

"Then we better get started."

Cole nods. "We should head to the bridge first and talk to the captain."

"Alright, let's do that now."

We make our way straight to the bridge, and unlike Cole and me, Ben looks like he managed to get some decent sleep—though the dead and distant expression in his eyes says otherwise.

He's clearly exhausted and sleep-deprived.

The corners of his handsome face sag, his jaw clenched tight, and a crease marks his brow.

Ben's face makes me want to lean forward and offer him a hug, whispering: "There, there. It'll be alright."

"Good morning to my two favorite people on board," Ben acknowledges us weakly.

Cole and I mumble a plain greeting back. "Good morning, Captain."

Cole strides into the room, carrying his laptop with him, where we've saved a copy of the footage. "We have something to show you."

Ben watches intently as we play the entire clip—from the kitchen to the lower hallway with the blind spot.

Afterward, his expression darkens. "So, it's one of the ship's employees?"

I'd prefer not to jump to conclusions. "Or it could be a passenger who put a crew member up to it. We can't isolate this case to just the kitchen staff."

Ben looks at me with a glimmer of trust. "You think so?"

"Yes," I confirm. "We've been up all night trying to establish connections between the people on the ship and Eleanor, both staff and passengers. We've finished going through the employee side and are halfway through the passengers, and we haven't made a solid connection yet. So, I wouldn't jump to that conclusion just yet."

"What are we supposed to do, then?" Ben searches between us for answers. "We have an upcoming port of call in Dover within a few hours."

Since I've spent considerable time learning cruise ship jargon, I understand that a port of call means a stopover where passengers can disembark for a day or two.

I shake my head. "Well, at this rate, we can't let anyone off the ship. We have no idea who did this; it could be anyone."

"We still have to stop at Dover to notify the authorities about Eleanor's death. We need to have her body retrieved, too."

"So, we'll stop at Dover, let the police take her body, and then everyone else stays onboard."

Cole joins the conversation. "How are we going to explain that? Tell them a passenger died on board and that everyone's a suspect?"

"Of course not," Ben replies. "We'll have to downplay it. I know how to handle that, so leave the announcements to me. For now, I need you both to interview the kitchen staff about this. I'll have the ship's legal team draft confidentiality agreements, so don't worry about being candid with them about the murder."

Cole and I nod in agreement.

I also reassure Ben, "We'll quickly establish connections and motives so we can let the others off at the next port. I promise."

Ben offers a soft smile. "Alright, thank you."

Cole and I set up our interrogation rooms—Cole using his office in the security room, while I stick to the small conference room Ben has generously lent us for the investigation.

Even Stacy is helping.

Instead of enjoying her luxury vacation, she's in my room, looking up the remaining passengers for any hint of a connection with Eleanor.

Before we start our investigations, Ben asks me to join him in talking to Dale about moving Eleanor's body at the next port.

We find Dale at the Solstice Bar, sipping a Cuba Libre at seven in the morning.

What a strong breakfast choice.

Dale doesn't seem too pleased to see us.

As we approach him, Dale greets us with a sharp edge in his voice. "Isn't it a compliment for the captain of the ship to visit someone personally? What do I owe this pleasure, Captain? Another 'I'm-sorry-for-your-loss' speech?"

"Calm down, Dale." I step in quickly. "We're doing our best to solve this case."

Thankfully, the Solstice Bar is empty this morning, apart from a mother and son wandering around the pool area and a few guests snapping photos of the view.

Dale shrugs dismissively. "And solving this case involves talking to me? Oh, right! I almost forgot I'm a suspect."

Ben speaks with authority. "If you cooperate with us, Mr. Bridges, you won't be a suspect for long."

"Sounds...exciting," Dale replies sarcastically. "What is it now? Where was I last night?"

"We're not here to interview you today," Ben replies, nodding at me.

So, I take over. "Dale, we came to inform you that in an hour, we'll be handing over Eleanor's body to the Dover Police."

"What?" Dale looks as though I've just punched him in the gut. "You can't do that. My family will come to pick her up—"

Ben explains, "Your family can pick up her body in Dover. We'll coordinate with the police regarding the investigation. I spoke with the station captain, and he agrees that the investigation should continue here on the ship—at least until we have a list of suspects. We just wanted to give you a heads-up."

Dale considers this for a moment. "Alright. Then, I'm getting off at Dover with her."

"I'm sorry, Mr. Bridges. You can't."

"What? What do you mean?"

"Like you said, you're a...suspect. We don't have enough information yet to pin this on anyone, so everyone's a suspect. No one is leaving the ship."

Dale stares at us in disbelief, then scoffs. "This is ridiculous. You can't keep me here!"

"We're not keeping you here," Ben explains. "We just need you to stay on the ship for the investigation."

"And the police agreed to this?"

"Yes," Ben replies, his tone apologetic. "They won't take over until we can present suspects and adequate evidence. So, I'm sorry."

Dale stands up from his stool, taking a step away from us. Before he completely disappears, he curses under his breath.

Chapter 12

"Everything's alright," I tell another group of tourists who look visibly disappointed at the news they can't disembark the Midnight Tide. "We just need to find the...missing object first."

This is what Ben announced thirty minutes before we arrived at Dover, England's port: that an important 'object' is missing, and no one can get off the ship until it's located.

I completely understand why the passengers are upset—no one wants to miss a chance to explore Dover Castle. As a compromise, we promise the cruise ship will sail by the iconic White Cliffs.

Now, that's a sight they shouldn't miss.

Everyone has something to say about this fabricated scenario; some are quick to blame one another. Others are just furious that they can't disembark. A few don't care—petty theft can't ruin their vacations.

In the meantime, I assure everyone we'll stay right on track, carefully omitting the part where we're actually trying to find suspects in a murder case before we let everyone off when we reach Scotland.

One passenger asks me, "What object is it? Maybe we can help find it, then we can get off the ship."

I chuckle uncomfortably. "Oh, no. We can't ask the passengers to do that. Captain's orders."

An older woman chimes in, her voice slightly louder than the rest. "I heard someone died on board. Is that true?"

The small group around me gasps and begins murmuring among themselves.

I manage to suppress a wince at her blunt and very true statement. "What? Of course not. Who said that?"

She replies, "Oh, my daughter overheard a young man talking about his relative's death on the ship—I presume that's why we can't get off."

Dale, I sigh internally.

As we speak, I spot Cole whispering something to his security personnel.

I assume they're moving Eleanor's body through the crew exit below so no passengers will notice.

I shake my head and laugh a little. "Oh, no. He's probably talking about another ship—we only have a missing display here."

"Oh, goodie!" The woman brightens up. "Well, do you at least have something planned for us today?"

"Of course," I say, forcing a smile. I scramble for something to say because I didn't plan any other events for today aside from passing by the White Cliffs.

So, relying on the research I did on our ports of call, I say, "We're...preparing a Dover-inspired teatime this afternoon, complete with some of Dover's best delicacies! Like...steak-and-ale pie and cream and jam scones!"

The passengers exclaim with delight before dispersing to the various rooms of the ship.

Phew. Now I just have to convince Ben to arrange for steak-and-ale pies and cream and jam scones to be delivered to the ship.

That, on top of everything else he has to worry about.

I should probably apologize in advance.

As I walk around, I hear a familiar bark growing closer. Turning to my right, I see Rex sprinting toward me, his short legs moving fast and his long ears flapping with each bounce.

I bend down to catch him. "Rex! What is it, buddy?"

He wags his tail enthusiastically, barking at me and pointing his nose in the direction from which he came.

I know he wants to take me somewhere.

I stand up and look around; since no one needs me at the moment, I turn to Rex. "Let's go, buddy. Lead the way."

Rex jogs back, glancing back at me to make sure I'm right behind him.

Thankfully, his little legs mean I don't have to run in heels.

But I'm unsure where he's taking me.

We make a few turns until we reach the hallway just outside the dining hall and the kitchen.

The path Rex is leading me on feels oddly familiar.

After a few minutes, I realize where we are—the same route that the person from the kitchen took after poisoning Eleanor's meal!

"Where are we headed, buddy?" I whisper to Rex as we continue along the path I remember from the security footage.

Finally, we turn into the narrow hallway—the one without a security camera.

This hallway leads to the crew cabins. Just a few more turns and flights of stairs, and I realize this is a more discreet route to the crew cabins.

While I expect Rex to take me down there, he stops in front of a utility closet, sniffing at the small opening beneath the door and scratching his paws against the heavy door.

I respond to his cues by opening the door.

There's nothing out of the ordinary inside—just a mop, a vacuum, some buckets, and a shelf filled with cleaning products.

A few trash bags are scattered around.

The closet is cramped enough; even standing inside feels claustrophobic. Still, Rex steps inside, following his nose to the corner where a pile of tied trash bags sits.

I watch him closely.

He sniffs around the bags a few more times before he zeroes in on one, biting into it and tugging it out of the pile with determination.

I decide to help him pull the bag.

Crouching beside Rex, I see the eagerness in his eyes; he wants me to open it. So, I reach down and untie the black plastic bag.

I quickly realize how sloppily it's tied—almost rushed. Ripping it open isn't hard at all.

Inside, I find a white fabric bundled up in a sloppy ball.

Studying it, I immediately recognize it as a uniform. But not just any uniform—a kitchen staff uniform.

My first thought is: what the hell is it doing in a utility closet?

Followed by: crap...it's the one the killer used, isn't it?

My heart races in my chest, pounding loudly in my ears, but I refuse to let my anxiety overwhelm me.

I scan the area and find a small clean towel. I wrap it around my hand before pulling the fabric out, wanting to avoid leaving any trace of my DNA.

With the towel, I lift the first piece of fabric to my eyes. I quickly realize it's a chef's jacket—complete with navy-blue lining on the flaps that marks it as part of the Midnight Tide's attire.

I check the jacket for a name tag, but find none.

Next, I inspect the pants, feeling the pockets to see if there's anything hidden there—maybe the poison itself. That would certainly be convenient for our investigation.

But despite the hasty way I found this uniform, there's no name tag and no poison bottle.

I even check the trash bag itself, but it's empty.

The uniform, if I had to guess, is a medium—which means it could belong to a man or a woman. Even Dale could fit into this uniform.

But if he was in the dining hall when it happened, that means he couldn't have slipped the poison into her meal. Still, it doesn't rule him out entirely.

He still has a motive—inheritance.

And that motive feels far more significant than embarrassment.

I should really go back and update the whiteboard.

For now, I place the clothes back into the trash bag and turn to my phone to call Ben. But before I can do that, Rex jumps on my leg with a whimper.

Once more, he tries to communicate with me.

I rub his ears. "What is it now, buddy?"

Rex sniffs the trash bag at my feet before heading back out into the hallway, his snout and entire body pointing in the same direction.

I stare at him, trying to decipher his intent. Then he barks at me, a command in his tone.

Talk about a language barrier.

Rex barks again before looking toward the narrow hallway that leads back to the crew cabins.

I do my best to interpret his actions.

Considering he sniffed out the clothes first, a wild thought crosses my mind—could Rex be leading me to the owner of this uniform?

The very person who could be the killer?

Since we don't have a forensic team to analyze this evidence, I decide at the last minute to let Rex take the lead from here.

I close the trash bag again and set it aside to return to later. I'm certain that if we examine this evidence closely, we'll find traces of maitotoxin woven into its threads and fibers.

For now, I'm determined to track down the owner of this uniform.

Thankfully, my miniature bloodhound helps me navigate swiftly toward the crew cabins.

There's nothing discreet about my sudden visit; the staff seems startled to see the cruise director wandering around their deck.

The crew cabins have two levels for lodging and amenities. The lower deck is reserved for the night shift crew since the cafeteria, lounge, and other common areas aren't located there—just bedrooms and the shower facilities.

Rex leads me down a particular hallway until he finally stops in front of a door labeled 2B-4.

I look into his motivated, beady eyes. "Is this it, buddy? Is this where the uniform is from?"

Rex gives me a small bark, almost inaudible—but it's a yes.

So, I glance at the room number and dial Stacy's number. She picks up immediately. "Rosie, what's up?"

I respond quickly. "Stace, are you in my room right now?"

I hope she is—the primary list of crew members, staff, and passengers is there, along with their background information for our investigation.

"You bet I am," Stacy answers with a yawn. "I'm still running additional checks on some passengers. I haven't found anything interesting yet."

"No, that's fine. But I need you to do something quickly."

"Sure! What is it?"

"I need you to find out who is the staff member staying in the crew cabin with room number 2B-4."

"2B-4?" I can hear papers shuffling on the other end of the line. "Let me check...2B-4."

I wait for a few moments, my gaze locked on the small door signage, feeling the tension mount.

Finally, Stacy responds. "Ah, found it! 2B-4 is currently housing four kitchen staff..."

Kitchen staff? Bingo.

"...and they're Josie Small, Marsha Flores, Kelsey Cho, and Melissa Russell."

"Can you send me all those names? I need to have a quick chat with Captain Anderson."

"Sure," Stacy pauses. "Can I ask what this is about?"

I step away from the door, worried that the killer might be listening as I speak.

Out of earshot, I inform Stacy, "We may need to sit down with those four girls because I just found a uniform stashed in a utility closet—the same one the killer wore that night when Eleanor was poisoned."

Chapter 13

Ben paces around the bridge, rifling through the files of each kitchen staff member currently lodged in crew cabin 2B-4.

Finally, he turns to Cole and me, who have been waiting patiently for him to say something since I informed him about the uniform I discovered during my "random inspection."

I can't exactly tell him my beagle led me to it, right?

"None of them have a connection to Eleanor, right?" Ben muses aloud, more to himself than to us. "I mean, I checked their records, and none of them have done anything criminal in their lives."

I offer Ben some reassurance, knowing he's been anxious and tense these past few days. "I'm sure there's a reason for all this, right?"

"Haven't we already interviewed these four girls?" he wonders aloud.

Cole reviews his checklist—the responsible one in this group. "No, not yet. We still have twelve people left on our list, including them."

"Good. Have them sign the NDA as well."

"Alright."

Ben glances at the plastic bag containing the discarded uniform. Then he turns to me, squinting. "How did you know that uniform belonged to one of the kitchen staff in 2B-4?"

Shit. I should've known this would come up.

I decide to wing it with a spoonful of truth. "My dog sniffed it out."

"Your dog?" Ben repeats, sounding incredulous. "Rex the beagle?"

I shrug, trying to play it cool. "I think his former owner trained him to be a bloodhound or something. I've been with Rex for three, four months now, and I can vouch that he knows what he's doing."

Ben and Cole exchange strange looks.

Feeling the need to defend my statement, I add—like an overripe cherry on top of a watery vanilla ice cream—"Once, Rex found my car keys when I thought I lost them. He found them under the couch."

Judging by their unimpressed expressions, I realize I should've come up with a better example.

Keys and murderers aren't exactly in the same league.

I blurt out, "Just...do you guys trust me?"

"Of course we do!" and "Absolutely!" overlap as answers. I guess I don't have to explain myself any further.

"Anyway," I start fresh. "We need to talk to those four girls. Since that area of the vessel has no security cameras, we need to go old school."

Cole mutters, "Old school, as in...waterboard them?"

We all burst into laughter at the joke.

Ben adds, "Or make them walk the plank, pirate-style!"

The laughter dies as quickly as it starts.

Then Ben's back to business. "I think it'd be best to ambush the four of them. Get them all in separate rooms at the same time, so no one talks to the others until they've all been interviewed."

I nod in agreement. "Sounds smart. Let's do that. I'll set up the conference room for now; we can interview them there."

Cole gets to work. "I'll round up the four kitchen staff. I'll bring them to you in about fifteen minutes."

"Sounds great." I stand up from my chair.

Ben informs us, "I'll join you a bit later. I have some things to wrap up."

"Got it, Captain. We'll see you soon."

With that, Cole and I leave the bridge, heading in opposite directions.

My task is straightforward: get one of them to confess. If not, find the most likely suspect.

As I exit, I run into Stacy outside the conference room.

She's wearing an under-eye mask infused with collagen and 24K gold. "I've been looking into so many people that I have terrible eye bags. I'm not always pretty, you know?"

I glance at her smooth face and rosy complexion, smiling. "Yeah, right!"

I push open the conference room door, and Stacy follows me inside. "But seriously, I've looked into almost a hundred people."

Turning to face her, I cup her cheeks in my hands. "If things get tough, just remember how utterly grateful I am for your help."

Stacy grins widely, mirroring my gesture as she squishes my face. "And that's why I do what I do."

Releasing me, she strolls over to one of the swiveling chairs and flops into it. "What's our agenda for today?"

"More interviews," I reply. "Rex did a great job and found some evidence that led us to today's...suspects."

Stacy sighs, her enthusiasm waning.

I flip the whiteboard around to show the clean side and push it aside.

Next, I prepare a pen and paper, anticipating I might need to jot something down. But knowing Cole, he'll probably handle that himself. He's what I'd call organized, if not a perfectionist.

Right on cue, Cole arrives with the first kitchen staff member—a small-faced woman with light blonde hair.

Josie Small—I recognize her from her photo.

Cole instructs Josie to sit comfortably before leaning in to whisper to me, "I asked security to keep an eye on the other three girls."

I nod, gesturing to an empty chair. "Sit with me."

Cole joins us at the table.

I open the interview. "Josie Small, right? You're one of the ship's assistant cooks."

Josie glances around at the three of us before answering hesitantly. "Y-yes, that's correct."

Cole slides the NDA toward her. "If you could, please sign here. It's a non-disclosure agreement. We just need to ensure no one discusses this conversation outside this room."

Josie looks nervous but signs the paper. "May I ask what this is about?"

With her signature on the NDA, I feel more confident about asking her the right questions. "It's regarding the death of a passenger onboard. We found evidence linking us to your crew cabin."

We proceed with standard questions—where was she the night of the murder, can anyone vouch for her alibi, and did she notice anything suspicious that evening?

Although Josie appears terrified, her answers are honest despite her shaking voice.

Being a private investigator has taught me how to read people's emotions.

Next up is Melissa Russell; she's more laid-back, almost casual about it. If it weren't for her nervous tick—scratching the hangnails on her thumbs—she might have seemed completely at ease.

So far, neither of them raises any red flags.

The third on our list is Kelsey Cho.

Unlike the others, Kelsey exudes a sense of dread—in an out-of-her-wits kind of way. She hesitates to sign the NDA and stutters through her answers, prompting us to pause and allow her to gather herself.

After Cole sets a bottle of water in front of her, I try again. "Kelsey, I know this situation is stressful, but you're not in trouble if you haven't done anything wrong. I'll ask you again: is there anything suspicious you want to tell us?"

Cole takes this as a cue for the good cop, bad cop routine—even if he fits the good cop role better.

He leans forward on the table. "Miss Cho, we know one of your kitchen uniforms is missing."

I glance at Cole, slightly alarmed at his boldness.

I remind myself that it's his first time investigating a murder—maybe he's been watching too many crime dramas. Either way, he deserves the benefit of the doubt.

To my surprise, Kelsey exhales a long, shuddering breath. "I—I swear I don't know how it happened; one of my uniforms went missing a few days ago."

Huh, Cole's tactic seems to be working. I can almost laugh.

Cole leans back, looking pleased with himself.

I continue, "What do you mean your uniform 'went missing?' Did it just...disappear from your closet?"

"Y-yeah, I mean, four employees share a room. We rarely lock the doors in case someone forgets their keys, you know?"

"So, you're saying anyone could come in and out of your room?"

"Yes! When I heard you were investigating the kitchen staff for a crime onboard, I immediately thought I'd be in trouble for that uniform."

"Then why didn't you report it missing?"

Her pupils tremble at my question. "Because...I was terrified it would make me look like a suspect."

And she does look like a suspect...

Kelsey has a convenient excuse—missing uniform and unlocked room.

I try to remain calm, even as my instincts are on high alert. "Alright, Kelsey. Thank you for your honesty. On that note, you don't mind if we check your room, right?"

Her face pales. "W-why?"

Cole and I exchange a curious look. I reply to Kelsey, "Just to ensure nothing else is out of place."

"You think...I did it, don't you?"

"Kelsey—"

"I didn't!" She erupts, her voice rising. "I swear. Please, I can't lose this job. I can't go to prison either. My mother is sick—"

Before her emotional breakdown reaches its peak, Stacy stands up from her chair, walks to Kelsey's side, and spins her chair to face her directly. "Kelsey, honey. Look at me."

Stacy uses her warm brown eyes and sisterly tone. "Nothing's going to happen to you. So, just calm down. They have to do this to clear your name. Do you hear me?

If you only misplaced your apron, then you're fine. Okay? You're fine."

I can't help but smile at Stacy's reassuring words.

She's always been my protector, even back in the Philippines when other little girls bullied me about my old gap tooth.

Out of the corner of my eye, I notice I'm not the only one charmed by this moment—Cole is, too.

By the time Kelsey calms down, someone knocks on the glass door.

I turn around and see Ben. I stand up, asking Cole to take over the investigation, then I step outside to meet Ben. "Captain, thanks for joining us."

"Sorry about the delay," he replies. "A 'mob' of passengers stopped me on the way, and I had to assure them that everything's fine."

"Been doing that all morning, too."

"And your pastries just arrived for our 'impromptu' English teatime."

"Sorry about that," I say with a brief smile.

"It's fine. So, what should we do now?"

"Well, one girl lost her uniform. I think it'd be best if we check their room for good measure."

"Okay, let's go."

We leave Cole to interview Kelsey and Marsha Flores. Meanwhile, Ben and I will investigate their room—and hopefully find a clue. Maybe even the poison bottle itself.

For safety measures, I hand Ben a pair of latex gloves I brought along.

I'm not entirely sure why I brought them, but now we're using them to avoid leaving prints in case this room holds relevant evidence.

When we arrive at crew cabin 2B-4, it's just like every other room—small, with two bunk beds, cabinets, and shoe racks. It's really tiny.

If all four staff members were standing, there wouldn't be much room to move around.

Searching through this space is quick and straightforward.

Ben and I divide the room between us, carefully examining the beds and cabinets for anything that could contain poison—something small, something that might still have traces of maitotoxin.

At least I hope it hasn't been destroyed, just like the uniform in the utility closet.

I check under the pillows and blankets, even feeling the mattresses for anything out of place. But I find nothing. In the closet, I roll up every pair of socks and check every pocket, but still, nothing.

It takes less than ten minutes for us to finish searching.

Ben scratches his eyebrow. "Well, nothing suspicious here. But I don't think that's a good sign either. For all we know, someone could have thrown the evidence overboard."

I nod in agreement. "That's my guess as well."

"So, does this clear Kelsey's name?"

Although Kelsey seems desperate, I don't entirely trust her story. So, I shake my head. "We should investigate her further before making that call."

Chapter 14

"Did you find anything?" I whisper to Cole as we stroll through the ship's theater, where we're hosting a consolatory movie night for the passengers since they can't leave the vessel today.

I decide on Pride & Prejudice for tonight's two screenings—something very…English.

Tomorrow morning, we'll show a kid's movie so the younger passengers can enjoy their turn, too.

Cole and I, along with other staff members, are checking the theater to ensure everything is clean and working properly.

"I'm still waiting for my colleague to send over Kelsey Cho's background information," Cole replies, sniffling as if he's caught a premature allergic rhinitis. "I asked him to look into everything. Don't worry about it."

I nod, shining a light down the aisles of the tidy auditorium seats. Not a popcorn kernel in sight. "How soon will we hear from him?"

"Anytime now."

"Well, alright."

After checking the theater, we begin assisting passengers as they enter, distributing popcorn and refreshments.

Allison approaches me, dressed to the nines in her Pride & Prejudice dreams, complete with a silk dress and patterned sheer gloves.

I immediately notice Dale awkwardly standing a few meters behind her.

Unlike Allison, Dale looks lazily dressed, just a white dress shirt and black jeans. He seems like someone who was coerced into being here.

Allison nudges me, sensing my gaze on Dale. "I heard about the…incident, I'm sorry. I thought it'd be best to get Dale 'out.' Since we can't leave the ship, we're just…here."

I smile softly at Allison. "Thank you. I think he needs some company now more than ever."

"Well, I'll make sure he gets out of his suite as much as possible."

"We'd appreciate that."

Allison gives my arm a brief, comforting rub. "We'll head inside now."

She turns to Dale, giving him a nod to follow her. Like clockwork, Dale trudges toward the entrance.

As he walks past me, I try to engage him in conversation. "Dale, how are you—"

He completely brushes me off as if I were a buzzing mosquito.

I can't blame him.

So instead of bothering Dale and his grief, I assist more passengers as they enter the theater.

A few minutes into the film, I see Cole jogging toward me, a paper in hand. He waves it in the air before handing it to me. "Fresh off the printer."

I take the sheet and skim through a comprehensive background check, detailing Kelsey Cho's primary education, work experience, and her family members' backgrounds.

Talk about thorough investigative work.

I quickly scan the pages, finding no links to Eleanor, her empire, or even the Bridges family.

At least nothing obvious.

I ask Cole, "Am I missing something? Is there something specific I should be looking for?"

Cole shakes his head. "Nothing in particular, no. On the surface, Kelsey doesn't seem to have any connection to Eleanor—unless it's personal."

"Like what?" I prompt him for his thoughts.

"I don't know," he admits. "But Eleanor wasn't exactly a likable woman."

Cole has a point.

Considering Eleanor's tactless mouth and unpleasant demeanor, she could easily have offended anyone aboard this ship.

But bringing maitotoxin onto the vessel seems intentional and targeted—it's not like you can just pick up contaminated shellfish on board.

Whoever did this has a personal vendetta against Eleanor.

Turning to one of the staff members, I excuse myself and suggest to Cole that we brainstorm together in the conference room one more time.

We look at the whiteboard, where I add Kelsey Cho as a suspected kitchen staff member.

Studying my scribbles on the board, I think out loud. "Dale has means, motive, and opportunity. Kelsey has evidence pointing toward her. Susie Lowe has motive and a foolproof alibi."

Cole stands beside me, his expression serious and contemplative. "I don't think Susie Lowe could've done it; she didn't have time to get poison after Eleanor boarded the vessel."

I agree, erasing Susie's name from the board. "I have this strong feeling we're missing something here."

"I know. Even Dale doesn't strike me as a murderous grandson."

"That doesn't mean he's innocent."

If we're relying solely on gut feelings, Dale should be at the top of our suspect list. Beyond his apparent grief, his potential inheritance sounds like a convenient motive. But as investigators, we need to focus on evidence and facts.

So, Dale remains on the board.

As Cole and I continue to connect the dots in our minds, we're interrupted by the sound of his phone ringing.

Even before Cole answers, I can tell the call is urgent.

I can sense it.

"Hester here," he says into the phone, pausing for a few seconds to listen. His face crumples into distress as he looks at me and repeats what he hears: "Kelsey Cho...overdosed?"

My eyes widen to the point where I almost think they'll pop out of my head. I lean away from the desk, holding my breath in anticipation of the next words from Cole's mouth.

Finally, he says, "We're on our way now."

Cole and I share an unspoken agreement to head to the infirmary as quickly as possible. We don't exchange words as we walk; I keep a few paces behind to let him lead the way, but I can tell we're heading to the infirmary.

When we arrive, Ben waits for us outside the hallway, flanked by two security personnel stationed at the entrance.

Ben perks up upon seeing us, already searching for answers. "Do you know what happened to Kelsey?"

Cole and I shake our heads. I reply, "Best we head inside to find out."

We enter the infirmary; it's a spacious room with a small reception area, a doctor's office, and several beds lined up in two columns.

Standing at the doorway of the doctor's office is the head doctor, Dr. Eve Lorenzo. She waves us over. "Right this way."

The three of us follow her into the small office.

In the corner of the room is another bed with the curtains drawn. As soon as we enter, Eve pulls the curtain aside, revealing what lies beyond the fabric.

To my horror, Kelsey is lying on the bed, her face pale and her lips dry and cracked.

"Is she okay?" I manage to utter, filled with concern.

Eve assures us, "Thankfully, she's stable."

"What happened?"

"She overdosed," Eve explains with a heavy sigh. "I've already run some blood tests, and while nothing conclusive has come back, it appears she overdosed on an antipsychotic medication. There are several in her system, but not enough to be lethal. Worst-case scenario, her heart could've stopped."

Hearing those words makes guilt churn in my stomach.

Part of me knows that this is my fault—I put her in a tight spot, and she tried to cope by taking a bunch of pills.

Was it also guilt that led her to do it?

Cole immediately chimes in, "What kind of pills? Because I've seen her medical records, and she wasn't prescribed any antipsychotics."

My melancholy shifts to curiosity.

Wait...is Cole suggesting Kelsey didn't do this herself?

"I can't say for certain," Eve replies. "What I can tell you is that not all medications are prescribed. Even opioids became widely available to the public in the 1990s. She could have obtained those pills from anywhere."

But we searched her room—and didn't find any pill bottles or anything similar. Unless she had taken it with her during her interrogation.

Still, I ask, "What if it wasn't hers and someone slipped it to her?"

Cole gives me a knowing look.

Ben interjects, "There are only two possibilities: either she did this out of guilt over Eleanor's death, or someone did it to silence her."

There's only one way to find out: we need to ask Kelsey.

So, I turn to Eve. "Doctor, when will Kelsey wake up?"

Eve gives me a look of uncertainty. "I can't say. It depends on the quantity and type of pills she took, as well as the dosage. All I know is that she'll be in and out of consciousness for a while."

"Can we talk to her when she wakes up?"

"I doubt it. She'll likely be too groggy to make sense of anything, let alone answer your questions coherently."

"Are you saying we have to wait a few days?"

"My best estimate is 48 to 72 hours. That's how long it might take for the medication to clear her system."

I can't believe it—we have to wait that long to get anything from Kelsey.

If Kelsey killed Eleanor, at least we don't have to worry about her fleeing. But if she didn't, we'll need to worry about the real killer getting away with it.

Not just escaping, but getting away with murder.

Chapter 15

The frustration etched on Ben's forehead deepens, a soon-to-be-permanent wrinkle forming.

Eleanor's death isn't just a personal tragedy; it's a legal nightmare for him as the ship's captain. I can see the sleepless nights taking their toll on him.

Cole and I are no strangers to this weight, either.

With a grieving grandson and a 'suicidal' kitchen staff, all we have left are motives and flimsy evidence—pitted between those two people.

It's no wonder I feel anxious this morning.

Ben has been fiddling with a gold coin for what seems like an eternity, a nervous tick that betrays his agitation. "We can't keep the passengers cooped up here forever," he says, frustration lacing his voice.

"I completely agree. We're almost at the port of Inverness, Scotland, right?"

"Right on schedule," he replies, his sigh heavy. "Which means we need to let the passengers disembark. We can't use the 'missing item' excuse twice at the next port."

I sense his anxiety matching my own; if we're wrong about Dale and Kelsey, we're handing the killer a free pass off this ship. But what else can we do? It's been four long days since Eleanor died on board.

Four days with no sign of the killer.

I attempt to lighten the mood with a poorly timed joke. "Well, if we let them go and the killer vanishes, at least that gives us more people to round up, right?"

Ben's chuckle is fleeting, barely a flicker of amusement. "To be sure, let's keep Dale and Kelsey on board—as if Kelsey could even get off the ship in her condition."

Kelsey's pale, fragile face from last night lingers in my mind.

At least Cole is checking in on her periodically.

I turn back to Ben. "Kelsey woke up this morning; Dr. Lorenzo managed to get her to eat a little before she dozed off again."

"So, she's not ready for another interrogation, then?"

"Not until she's fully awake. We can't trust anything she says in her drugged state."

"Fantastic," Ben mutters, sarcasm thick in his voice.

I reach for his hand, wanting to stop him from endlessly toying with the coin. "Hey, we're going to figure this out, okay?"

He squeezes my hand, a brief moment of connection. "I hope so, Rose."

In that instant, the world falls away. The ship's mechanical hum fades, the water's gentle slapping against the hull disappears, and it's just Ben and me—until someone clears their throat.

Ben and I jerk away from each other, startled.

His first mate stands there, a weak smile on his face. "Sorry to interrupt, Captain, but we're nearing the port at Inverness. I wanted to know what message to send out to the passengers."

Ben stands abruptly, discomfort flashing across his face.

It's not like we were caught in an intimate moment, but it sure feels that way.

Damn it, I should have taken more time to date in my early twenties instead of feeling this awkward around a handsome man.

Ben replies, "We're sticking to the original plan; let the passengers know they can disembark from 8:00 a.m. to 5:00 p.m."

"Understood, Captain." The first mate's smile grows as he turns to leave.

I suddenly stand, my knee colliding with the table—a perfectly awkward moment. "I'll—I'll go talk to Dale."

Without waiting for Ben's response, I rush out. He quickly follows, saying, "Not alone; I'll come with you."

I want to protest, but doing so would only highlight my attraction to him, so I keep quiet.

We greet staff and passengers as we make our way to Dale's suite, a route that has become all too familiar.

Knocking on his door feels routine now.

After a few moments, it swings open, revealing Dale's sullen face. "Great, it's you two again. Let me guess, I can't get off the ship?"

"How did you know—" I start, my eyebrows furrowing.

"The announcement," he says, stepping back to let us in, flopping onto the couch. "I heard the passengers can 'deboard.' But you two showing up again means I'm stuck here."

We're really testing our luck with Dale.

Ben enters the room, his demeanor serious. "We're very sorry, Mr. Bridges. But until we clear your name, you must remain on the ship."

"What part of 'I didn't kill my grandmother' don't you get?" Dale snaps, frustration spilling over.

"Evidence," Ben replies flatly, maybe bluffing a bit. We don't exactly have any concrete proof against Dale.

I jump in, "We know there are inheritance issues with Eleanor in your family."

Dale laughs bitterly. "Right, because tabloids are so trustworthy."

I want to argue, but the internet is just a cesspool of nasty gossip. Instead, I say, "Regardless, you have to stay on the ship."

Dale fixes us with a predatory gaze. "Shouldn't you be asking if I want a lawyer? Because I'm starting to feel like a suspect in this whole mess."

Ben shoots back, "It's not like that—"

Just then, the door swings open, and Allison walks in, her expression neutral. "Sorry to interrupt, but I overheard your conversation from the hallway. I thought this should be private."

Ben glances at me, his concern evident. I murmur, "She knows. Dale must have told her."

Ben visibly relaxes, his shoulders dropping. "Oh, alright then."

Dale looks to Allison for support. "Tell me, Allison, isn't this completely absurd? They want to lock me up on this ship."

I try to calm him. "Dale, it's not like that. You need to understand—"

"Understand what!?" He jumps to his feet, pacing the room, frustration radiating from him. "I didn't do any-thing wrong! All I want is to leave this goddamn ship!"

Allison senses the tension and steps in, guiding Dale toward the bedroom. "I'll stay with you, alright? Just breathe."

Once she's gotten Dale settled, she returns to us, her gaze apologetic. "I don't want to interfere with your jobs, but you should cut him some slack; he just lost his grandmother."

I assume she's speaking to Ben, so I let him respond. "We just have to keep him here until we find solid evidence."

"Then do it faster," Allison says, her tone shifting to urgency. "Sorry, I just feel terrible for Dale. He hasn't told his family yet; he's afraid they'll blame him. If anyone wants to clear his name, it's him."

Allison has too much faith in Dale for someone who barely knows him. Either she's incredibly trusting or just naïve.

But I don't judge; I just hope Dale won't disappoint her.

Right now, I need to clear his name.

"How about this," Allison suggests. "I'll keep an eye on Dale; make sure he doesn't cause any trouble. In exchange, just let him off the ship. He needs to breathe."

I glance at Ben for his thoughts.

Just as he opens his mouth to speak, Dale storms out of the bedroom and grabs Allison's wrist. "You don't need to bargain with them. Come on."

Allison can't protest; he's already dragging her away, casting a brief glance back at us.

As their footsteps fade, Ben and I are left standing in the now-empty suite.

"What now?" Ben asks, staring at the empty hallway.

I look around the space, feeling alde weight of the situation. "I guess we should leave for now."

Ben nods in agreement, and we head for the door. Just as I step out, I hear a phone ringing from somewhere nearby.

The sound halts me. "Wait..."

Ben turns back as I scan the room for the source of the noise, but I find nothing.

It must be close.

Following my instinct, I step back inside, and Ben asks, "What are you doing?"

"Following the sound," I reply, zeroing in on the ringing.

Ben doesn't question me further; he stands by the doorway, keeping watch as I snoop around.

I trace the ringing to the couch, where a black phone is wedged between the cushions.

I retrieve it just as the call ends.

The screen lights up at my touch, revealing a screensaver photo of Eleanor with a baby—perhaps her great-grandchild.

I glance at the screen, and a realization hits me: this could be golden evidence in our murder investigation.

Turning to Ben, I hold it up. "Look what I found."

Chapter 16

Inverness is a stunning city on Scotland's northeast coast, draped in lush greenery and framed by rolling hills and old stone structures that remind me of a Viking movie.

After five long days at sea, my feet finally touch solid ground. I feel... balanced. Stable. Unlike on the ship, where my knees wobbled with every wave.

"This is an adventure!" Stacy squeals beside me, bundled in her turtleneck and coat—it's a brisk 59 degrees Fahrenheit.

I can't help but chuckle at the wonder in Stacy's wide eyes, forever reflecting her childlike innocence—one of her sweeter traits.

I tease her, adopting a flat tone. "It's not an adventure, Stace. We just need to unlock Eleanor's phone. Thankfully, Ben has a contact here."

I can't help but ponder how part of Ben's job seems to be knowing people everywhere.

Once we find Eleanor's phone, Ben offers to call someone on the island to assist us.

So here we are.

"Boo!" Stacy suddenly exclaims. "You don't have to be a buzzkill about it."

I laugh. "Fine. I'll let you have your fun while we're here, as long as we get this one important thing done."

"Oh, we should take photos for Inay and Itay!"

"Yeah, sure!"

If I'm being honest, I haven't thought about our parents much lately—guilty as charged. Maybe even bordering on terrible daughter territory. But we do keep in touch.

I promised to call them after my first cruise as director.

Fortunately, Stacy loves keeping our parents updated. So, as she stretches her arm for a selfie, I flash my best smile.

No murders on this cruise—that's the smile I aim for.

After snapping a photo with the Midnight Tide behind us, Stacy and I stroll down the port.

We hail a cab and direct the driver to the address Ben gave us earlier.

Though my visit to this island is strictly for evidence-gathering, I can't help but enjoy the scenic views of the cozy town. Every route is picturesque.

The driver drops us off at a stunning home perched on a cliff, overlooking the glimmering River Ness.

I find myself staring into the sparkling waters, imagining a long, scaly creature gliding beneath the surface.

Maybe that's how the Loch Ness monster legend began.

Stacy approaches the stone porch of the modern-looking house, half-glass and half-concrete, with a lovely blend of white and brown paint.

I catch up with her, and we ring the doorbell.

The door swings open almost instantly to reveal a tall, muscular guy with glasses.

A real Clark Kent type.

"Ben's friends?" he asks.

"Yes," I reply. "I'm Rose, and this is Stacy. We work for the Midnight Tide."

"I'm Jay." He opens the door wider, gesturing us inside. "Come in and make yourselves at home."

The interior screams luxury, with glass decorations and sparkling chandeliers that catch the light.

We're immediately greeted—not so warmly—by a plump, furry white Persian cat that stretches languidly on the carpet.

Jay points to her. "That's Lottie."

Stacy drops to her knees, cooing at the cat. "Hi there, Lottie."

Jay turns to me. "Can I get you anything?"

I shake my head. "No, we're fine. It's enough that you're doing us a huge favor."

I pull out Eleanor's phone from my sling bag and hand it to Jay. "Here it is."

He takes the phone and studies it for a moment. "Alright, I hope you don't mind waiting for about half an hour."

"Oh, don't worry about us. We're fine."

"The kitchen is that way," he points to the hallway on the left. "Bathrooms are the first door to the right."

I nod. "Thank you. But really, we don't need much."

"Alright then. Hope you enjoy the view."

I turn to the glass wall, the river stretching before us, breathtaking, with an outdoor patio and a fireplace that beckons.

I wonder if Jay is more than just a tech nerd—maybe he's a tech millionaire.

Once Jay exits, Stacy turns to me, eyes wide with excitement. "This place is incredible!"

I can't help but agree. "It really is."

Stacy glides toward the floor-to-ceiling glass window and slides the door open. "Come on!"

I hesitate, feeling a bit awkward wandering around someone's home without their presence, but we're not breaking in, so I join her outside, letting the wind hit my face.

Stacy and I decide to wait outside for Jay.

At one point, he checks in on us, balancing cups of coffee and store-bought muffins in his hands, before retreating back to his office to work on unlocking Eleanor's phone.

Like clockwork, exactly 32 minutes later, Jay reenters the living room with Eleanor's phone in hand. "Here it is."

I take the phone, and Jay says, "I disabled the security features, so you can access it whenever you want. Feel free to restore it later if you wish."

I check the phone, relieved to find myself on the home screen—no more passwords or fingerprint scans. "Thank you, Jay."

"No problem," he replies with a smile. "I just hope Ben isn't up to anything illegal with that phone."

"Oh, no, he's not," I laugh lightly. "It belongs to a passenger."

"Old woman who forgot her passcode?"

"Y-yeah, something like that."

It's not exactly true, but Jay's assumption is much simpler than the reality.

Finally, I say, "Well, thanks for helping us out. We owe you one."

"No, no. I owe Ben, so this is nothing."

I'm almost tempted to ask what Ben did for him, but I don't pry. "Well, we should be on our way."

Jay walks us to the front door. "Thanks for stopping by. Send Ben my regards."

"Will do," I reply as Stacy and I step out of the house.

Once outside, Stacy turns to me. "Would it be alright if I go ahead to the ship? I want to explore a bit and try some local dishes while I'm here. I'm still on vacation, you know."

I laugh, feeling slightly ashamed for dragging my sister along on official business. "Of course! I'll see you on the ship."

"I'll bring you back some souvenirs and snacks."

"Sounds like a deal."

After walking down the hill, Stacy and I part ways, taking separate cabs—I head back to the port as quickly as possible.

As I sit in the back of the cab, I can't help but sift through Eleanor's phone. Having it in my possession is too tempting.

I'm sure Ben wouldn't mind if I took a peek.

So, while I ride back to the port, I access Eleanor's phone.

The first thing I check is her call logs. Everyone she called, and who called her, seems familiar—nothing suspicious.

As much as I feel for Eleanor, going through her phone is crucial for solving her murder. I swallow the guilt building in my throat and move on to her messages.

It doesn't take long to spot something alarming.

Apart from a few unopened messages from people Eleanor knew, there's a message from an unknown number sent on the night of her murder.

I click on the message thread.

What I find chills me—a series of one-sided messages from the unknown number—seven in total—starting the moment the Midnight Tide set sail.

I read them chronologically.

"Welcome aboard your last cruise"—a clear threat.

"There you are again with your nasty temper."

I glance at the timestamp; it's just moments after Eleanor publicly humiliates an attendant.

My throat tightens with each new message.

"Ignoring me, huh? Too OLD to play games?"

"Your grandson seems to adore you. What a shame he won't get to adore you much longer."

The messages come in at different times throughout the day.

By evening, Eleanor receives two final messages. One before dinner: "3, 2, 1..."

Is this person counting down to her death?

And the last message: "I see you."

I feel nauseous as I absorb the implications.

Seven threatening messages that Eleanor ignored are now the last messages she ever received.

All the more reason to keep the passengers on the ship—one of them is the killer.

But who?

Considering they refer to Dale as "your grandson," it seems he's likely innocent.

Yet this discovery offers no comfort.

One thing is clear: vengeance lies at the heart of this murder.

Chapter 17

"What are we going to do now?" Ben throws the dreadful question into the air for Cole and me to absorb. His gaze flickers to Eleanor's phone again. "This doesn't look like something Dale sent, and I can't imagine Kelsey sending them either. So, we might have let the killer slip off the ship to escape."

"Don't say that," I quickly interject, hoping not to jinx anything. "If this killer is smart, they'll return to the ship. We just have to keep them thinking they're getting away with it. At least until we catch them."

Cole sighs beside me. "But it could be anyone. Can't we just call the phone?"

I shake my head, knowing we need to tread carefully. "If we do that recklessly, we could tip off the killer. We have to be smarter than they are."

Ben adds, "Calling it means we're counting on that same phone still being on the ship."

Another dreadful thought crosses my mind—one that sends my heart sinking. "It's still hope. Assuming the phone is still with its owner, we must find it. Since the killer only disposed of the uniform, it's safe to assume the phone is still with them."

This time, Ben drops into a chair at our table, the weight of the situation palpable. "Which brings us back to the question: what are we going to do now?"

Cole and I exchange glances, pondering the right answer.

After a few seconds, an idea pops into my head. "We divide the passengers and the crew, then we call the phone. We can't keep searching through everyone; this way, we can narrow down the suspects."

Ben and Cole nod, and Ben replies, "Okay. But how do we do that?"

I look at him, expecting a wild reaction to my equally wild idea. "We host multiple events tonight to draw the passengers in. Then we'll scatter security personnel to ensure every phone ringing has someone observing it."

For a moment, Ben looks at me like I've lost my mind—maybe I have. "Multiple events? How many are we talking about?"

"How does a one-to-a-hundred ratio sound?"

"Expensive," Ben replies bluntly. "But necessary. So, these five events we're suddenly hosting—what exactly are they?"

I say the first things that come to mind. "Another movie night—we had great turnout last night. We can do it again."

"Okay, movie night. Then what?"

"Um... a live band at the Solstice Bar," I suggest, glancing at Ben and Cole. "But I'm open to other ideas."

Cole jumps in. "How about a stargazing event on the deck? We could rent a telescope or something."

Ben nods, jotting down notes mentally. "Since we're putting on random shows here, let's add an ice carving demonstration in the dining hall."

I chuckle at Ben's suggestion and throw out an absurd but doable idea. "Then we can have a stand-up comedy show in the recreational hall."

"Why not?" Ben raises his hand in the air, enthusiasm growing. "We need to bring all the passengers together, right? These events sound inviting to me."

Phew. Thankfully, Ben is easy to work with.

In return, I assure him, "I'll head back to the city to make these surprise events happen for tonight."

Cole adds, "I'll brief the security personnel about it. What time are we executing this plan?"

"At exactly 10:00 p.m.," I say firmly. "I'll call the number right on the dot."

Ben says, "I'll make the announcements to get everyone excited for tonight's events."

Now, it's all hands on deck.

With help from Stacy and Kellie, we manage the events despite the short notice.

Stacy secures a stand-up comedian and a live band, while Kellie finds a place to rent a telescope. I track down a professional ice carver before returning to the ship and setting up for another movie night.

We need as many people as possible to make everything work.

Thankfully, we do.

To streamline tracking, we set up a registration booth outside each event for passengers to sign in.

My only fear is that all this effort could be wasted if someone disposes of the phone. Our initial concern that the killer wouldn't return has faded; by five in the afternoon, all the passengers are back.

It's now 9:45 p.m., and everyone is in position. By 'in position,' I mean security personnel are stationed in hallways and crew areas. Cole is in the dining hall, where the largest event will be held.

Stacy is at the Solstice Bar, and Kellie is in the theater.

Meanwhile, Ben and I are in the security room, watching everything unfold through the cameras. We can't afford to miss a thing.

Ben is just as nervous as I am; I can see him massaging his hands restlessly. "It's going to work, right?"

I nod at the screens before us. "It has to. We didn't put in all this effort for nothing. I'm optimistic we'll have something by the end of the night."

"And if we don't...?"

"Then we keep looking."

Ben stares at me for a moment before finally chuckling softly.

I look at him curiously. "What?"

Ben smiles. "You just reminded me of the first time I saw you on the ship; you had that same fiery look in your eyes."

I feel warmth creeping into my cheeks, so I turn back to the screens. "Oh,"

Ben laughs again before focusing closely on the monitor. "We're just minutes away from finding the killer."

I glance at the wall clock. "Yep. We'll wait for most of the passengers to settle in."

For the next few minutes, Ben and I observe as passengers filter into their chosen events. The ice carving demonstration is attracting more attendees than the others.

Five minutes before ten, I radio all stations, asking for the turnout numbers.

The ice carving has 130 passengers, the stand-up comedy has 83, stargazing has 96, the theater has 105, and the live band has 65 passengers.

Twenty passengers didn't join any event, but that's nothing compared to 479 total.

Here's hoping the killer is one of those 479.

Three minutes before ten, I instruct the event coordinators not to start yet and to wait for my signal.

Silence is crucial for our plan to work—we need to hear that phone ring.

Two minutes, and my hand hovers over the phone, ready to dial the number that threatened Eleanor before her death.

One minute, and I whisper a prayer to the wind, hoping we catch a glimpse of the killer tonight.

Five seconds...

Four, three, two...

And one—I tap the call icon on Eleanor's phone, and the security room falls into tense silence. Our breaths held.

Ring, ring, ring.

I hear it echoing from somewhere. This is proving harder than I expected.

Where is it coming from?

Ben quickly shifts his focus between the frames, trying to locate the source of the ringing.

One more ring, then click—the call disconnects.

I try again, but this time, the call doesn't go through; the killer has turned off the phone before we can pinpoint where the sound came from.

Fortunately, a voice comes in over the radio—it's Cole. "It came from the dining hall; I heard a phone ring the instant the clock struck ten."

The dining hall.

Ben answers through the radio. "Are you sure, Cole?"

"Absolutely, Captain," Cole replies confidently.

I take the radio from Ben to instruct Cole. "Cole, I need you to secure the registration list. The killer's in there."

"Got it. I'll bring it to the security room right away."

"Thank you,"

As I return the radio to Ben, he looks at me with hopeful anticipation. "Does this mean we're close to finding the killer?"

I nod, a shadow of a smile playing on my lips. "Yes, but there's still a long way to go. For now, we're 369 people closer to the culprit. Only 130 passengers to focus on."

Ben nods. "Better than 499."

Chapter 18

Stacy walks around the conference room, delivering cups of coffee to Cole, Ben, and me, fully aware that we're in for another long night.

At this point, I'm pretty sure 50% of my blood is caffeine.

Cole is busy in the corner, connecting his laptop to the projector so we can review the security footage from 10:00 p.m., right when someone's phone rings.

Ben and I are taking turns skimming through the registration list of 130 passengers.

Ben's frustration is palpable. "There's no way we can investigate 130 passengers before we dock at Lerwick—that's nine hours away. If we don't pinpoint the killer tonight, we risk letting them slip away again. Maybe this time for good."

"We'll find the killer," I assure him. "Stacy already finished reviewing the passengers' backgrounds; all we need to do now is connect those dots to Eleanor, her family, and her empire."

Stacy claps the pile of papers she prepared for us, detailing the 130 passengers and their basic backgrounds. "I'm not saying this is foolproof, but it might help."

Cole chimes in. "Who knows? Maybe we'll even catch the killer on camera."

He clicks the projector remote, and the screen lights up with a paused frame from tonight's ice carving event at the dining hall. It's a high vantage point, so we can see about 70% of the room.

Even before Cole clicks play, I spot several people on their phones. After all, they were there to witness the ice carving demonstration—maybe even record it or snap some photos.

Finally, Cole presses play with the timestamp at 9:59 p.m., just enough for us to scan the frame for potential suspects. It's not easy.

I squint at the screen, struggling to make out any faces. Thankfully, I'm not alone; three other pairs of eyes are glued to the video.

We all hold our breaths, eager to hear everything.

Sixty seconds tick by, and the recorded ringing starts to echo in the dining hall. With loud chatter and the whir of machines, it's nearly drowned out.

Ring, ring, ring.

A few heads turn toward their phones—too many to keep track of. From this distance, it's impossible to identify anyone.

Ring. Ring...then silence.

Ben orders, "Can you play that back for at least ten seconds?"

Cole complies, rewinding the video. We listen intently until the ringing noise returns, and Ben stands closer to the projector screen, his eyes narrowing.

"There," he points to a man seated at one table. "Who's that guy?"

Cole hits pause just as the guy turns sideways, revealing only half his face.

I lean in closer, but I can't recognize him either.

Then Stacy squeals, "Oh! Oh! I know this guy; let me find him in the pile."

We all turn to her as she quickly flips through the pages of her notes. Finally, she extracts a three-page sheet from the stack. "Here he is! I've been working with the passenger list long enough to recognize names."

I high-five Stacy. "I never doubted you for a second."

Ben takes the sheet from her. "Let's keep doing this; we need to look for anyone who glanced at their phone and hung up at the same time."

"Okay," I nod, turning to Cole with intent. "Play the video back."

Cole rewinds it again, and we all point at different figures, trying to identify them amidst the pixelated frames.

The phone rings again, and I spot a woman in her mid-40s or early 50s checking her phone. "That one," I say, pointing.

Cole pauses it again, and Stacy quickly adds another sheet to our growing pile.

We continue like this.

We're accurate about four out of five times—there's still one person we can't identify even after multiple replays. So, we snap a photo and move on to the next individual.

How many people had to be on their phones when I made that call?

Eight people later, Ben's phone rings.

He answers immediately, not even glancing at the caller ID. "This is Captain Anderson."

Ben listens intently, his expression shifting to surprise. "We'll head there right now, doctor. Thank you."

When he pulls the phone away from his ear, I can't help but ask, "Is everything okay?"

Ben nods slowly, clearly weighing his words, then finally tells me, "Kelsey just woke up. Dr. Lorenzo says she's conscious, and we can talk to her if we want."

I realize I've almost forgotten about Kelsey—I've been so caught up running around all morning that I haven't checked on her.

But if she's awake now, that's a good sign; we weren't expecting her to regain consciousness until tomorrow at the earliest.

I glance around the room at Cole's worried face and Stacy's big brown eyes, knowing we need to act. "Let's go see Kelsey."

The four of us rush into the clinic, where Kelsey is sitting on a cot, an IV drip still attached to her hand.

Dr. Lorenzo stops us before we reach her. "She's conscious enough to talk now; I think the fluids helped flush the drugs out of her system."

Ben responds, "Thank you, doctor."

"You're welcome," she says, gesturing toward Kelsey. "Now, you better talk to her if you want to find who you're looking for."

We approach Kelsey's bed, and she turns to us with wide, scared eyes. "Captain, Miss Dela Cruz..."

"How are you feeling, Kelsey?" I whisper.

But our presence seems to make her more anxious; she scans us all, uncertainty flickering in her gaze.

Stacy takes it as a cue to excuse herself and Cole. She touches my elbow gently. "We'll wait for you in the conference room."

Cole, entranced by Stacy's beauty, doesn't argue. "We'll keep watching the video."

I nod at them. "We'll join you once we're done here."

I turn back to Kelsey, who seems to relax a little now that there are fewer people. "Sorry about that. So, how are you feeling, Kelsey?"

"Slightly lightheaded," she admits. "But I think I'm okay."

Ben asks, "Do you know what happened to you and why you're here?"

"Am I still in trouble?" Her glassy eyes betray her innocence; she didn't attend tonight's events, freeing her from suspicion.

I shake my head. "No, you're not. And we're sorry for putting you in this situation."

"Did you find the...killer?"

"No, we haven't," I sigh, wishing I could say otherwise. "But I think you can help us find them. We believe they're connected to why you're here—I mean, if you didn't do it to yourself."

"You mean drug me?"

"Y-yeah, so you know what happened to you?"

"Yes," Kelsey replies, fear evident in her expression.

"Can you tell us what happened?"

Kelsey nods. "I was on my break that night. I went to my cabin to rest and drink some water. But after a few seconds, I felt...dizzy. Like I was going to collapse. And I did. Didn't I?"

"Yes," Ben answers gently. "I'm sorry you had to go through that."

It pains me to inform Kelsey, but I need her on our side. "You weren't just drugged, Kelsey; someone gave you a potent dose of antipsychotics. A few more of those, and your heart would've stopped."

Kelsey's eyes widen, her pupils dilating with fear. "You mean...someone tried to kill me?"

"Yes. We think it's the killer on board. I also suspect they wanted to frame you for the murder, making it look like a suicide."

Ben's expression turns serious. "Tell me, did anyone give you the water you drank that night?"

"No," Kelsey shakes her head. "It's from my water jug."

Suddenly, it hits me. "Kelsey, was that jug in your cabin? The same cabin you and your roommates rarely lock?"

"Y-yes, that's right."

"So, just like when you lost your uniform, are you saying someone could have entered your room and drugged your water? But how would they know it's your water?"

"I usually keep it right next to my bed. But... I'm not sure."

I mumble quietly, "But the killer is a passenger..."

How could they know the water jug belongs to Kelsey? Were they watching her closely to frame her? What kind of passenger has access to the crew cabins?

It's not adding up—we're missing something vital.

Ben asks Kelsey, "Do you know anyone who could've done this to you? Was there anyone suspicious—a passenger—who approached you?"

Kelsey thinks for a moment. "N-no. I don't remember anyone suspicious."

Is it really a passenger? I doubt my instincts. What if the killer knew we'd investigate the passengers and was leading us in that direction?

What if they're playing with us right now?

Ben notices my distress and places a comforting hand on my back. "Are you okay, Rose?"

I turn to him, forcing a smile. "Y-yes. Just thinking."

Kelsey then asks, "Could it be one of my roommates? Or maybe another crew member on the ship?"

It's a possibility—but one we had dismissed days ago. Especially now that we've confirmed it's a passenger.

But what if it wasn't?

What if a crew member had brought a phone to the dining hall?

But what if I'm wrong...

Focus, Rose. Now is not the time to doubt myself. It's the perfect moment to remember that when in doubt, trust your instincts.

And my instincts tell me it's a passenger. But how did they gain access to the crew cabins? It's not like they didn't have the opportunity the first time. This is yet another mystery to unravel along the way.

Chapter 19

Bark. Bark.

I hear Rex running on the deck of the Midnight Tide.

He's bounding around wildly, without reason or direction, just running blindly until he nears the edge of the ship.

"Rex!" I shout, panic tightening my chest at the thought of him tumbling into the midnight blue ocean. "Come back here!"

He barks one more time before losing his footing at the edge, and I scream.

I jolt awake from this nightmare, sweaty and heart pounding like a jackhammer. I sit up, scanning the dimly lit room.

Then I hear Rex barking again—just like in the dream. Except this time, he's scratching at the door, whimpering as he turns to me.

Running my fingers through my hair, I whisper to him, "Why are you still up, buddy? Do you need to go out?"

I glance at the bathroom door, slightly ajar to allow Rex easy access, but he continues scratching at the main door, eager to be let out.

Maybe he wants to go for a walk.

I turn to the clock on my bedside table and see it's 2:45 a.m.—far too early for his usual morning stroll, but Rex's whimpers are hard to ignore. I swing my legs over the side of the bed and grab some jogging pants from the cabinet.

"Alright, alright. I hear you." I tell him as I pull on my joggers. "We're going for a walk at this ungodly hour."

Rex spins in circles as I approach the door, as if thanking me.

The moment I open it, he barks one last time before darting out.

Just like in my dream where he falls into the water, I stifle a shout as I call his name, rushing after him.

"Not so fast, Rex!" I order, though my voice is lost on him. "You might fall!"

Rex races further up the vessel, leading me out of the cabins and into a hallway on one of the common decks, just one level below the passenger suites.

"Rex!" I half-shout behind him as he speeds into an open area, where only railings stand between him and the churning sea below.

Is my dream turning into reality? No. I can't let that happen.

I push myself to run faster, watching Rex's small frame as he veers toward the open side of the ship. My heart drops as I lose sight of him around a corner.

I hurry into the area where he disappeared.

Relief floods me as I hear his barking—except this time, it's aggressive. He's growling, and I quicken my pace to reach him.

The sound of the ocean crashing against the hull greets me, and the wind whips my hair in all directions.

I find Rex a few feet away, barking at something—or rather, someone.

Not just anyone, but Allison.

Allison looks annoyed at Rex's barking, but then her expression shifts to surprise as she sees me appear behind him.

I notice the thick jacket wrapped tightly around her. Her nose is red from the cold wind.

"Allison," I shout over the roar of wind and water. "What are you doing here?"

One of her elbows rests against the railing. Unlike me, her hair is neatly tied back, suggesting she hasn't been to bed yet. "Rose, what a pleasant surprise running into you here."

Rex continues to bark, so I close the distance and scoop him up in my arms. "Calm down, buddy."

Even cradled in my arms, Rex keeps growling at Allison.

I can't help but scan the empty, narrow walkway. Besides Allison and me, there's no one else around, and our only view is a distant lighthouse. Everything else is shrouded in darkness.

I look back at Allison. "We should probably get inside; it's safer there. I don't want you accidentally falling over the railings."

Allison nods and follows me inside the ship, where I shut the door behind us. "What are you doing out here?"

She looks at me as if she's puzzled by my question. "I... couldn't sleep, so I went out for a smoke."

I didn't take her for a smoker, but I keep that thought to myself.

Before I can respond, Rex wriggles out of my grip, returning to his barking stance as he glares at Allison. "I'm sorry about my dog. He's not usually like this."

Allison glances at Rex. "Don't worry about it. Dogs seldom like me."

She looks back up at me. "I'll head back to my room. I'll see you around the ship."

I nod slowly, an uneasy feeling gnawing at me.

The way Allison avoids making eye contact, how her hands seem restless, and her overall discomfort—it's as if I caught her doing something wrong, even though she claims to just be smoking.

"Okay," I reply as she turns to leave. "Good night."

Allison walks away, but then she suddenly stops. I wait for her to say something, but she hesitates before finally turning back to me. "You know what, Rose? I think there's something I need to tell you."

Her expression softens, turning serious. "It's about...Dale."

My eyebrows knit together; I didn't expect her to bring him up. She's always been protective of him, so discussing him behind his back feels unexpected.

I reply cautiously, "Oh, sure. What about him?"

Allison glances around, as if debating whether to speak. "Dale has been... how do I put this nicely? He's been acting differently."

"Differently?" I echo. "What do you mean?"

"I mean, he's... on edge." Allison struggles to articulate her thoughts. "I thought it was just his grief or anxiety about being a suspect. But he's... angrier. He's 'dying' to get off the Midnight Tide."

I can understand that; Dale likely wants to be with his grandmother for one last time.

I let Allison continue. "Last night, he told me that staying on the ship would only get him into more trouble."

She emphasizes the last word, suggesting something more. I ask, "Are you trying to say he could've done something—"

"No, no, no," Allison interrupts, laughter shaky. "I'm not going to do that to him. He's just grieving, and I want to believe he's a good guy. I think he is, don't you?"

She thinks Dale is a good guy—not knows.

It sounds like she's trying to convince herself. Like she's clinging to the hope that Dale didn't murder his grandmother.

I don't believe he did either. But does Allison know something?

Trying to make sense of her words, I say, "Allison, you know you can tell me anything, right? You don't have to dance around it; I'm listening."

"Right..." Allison takes a deep breath. "I don't want to betray him, but you're right, Rose. I think Dale did something to his grandmother."

Hearing those words sends chills down my spine, but it feels so wrong.

My goosebumps feel out of place.

In this moment, I'm convinced Dale isn't the killer. Even with motive, means, and opportunity, grief is a heavy burden that leaves marks on the soul. I felt Dale's grief.

Was I mistaken?

Instead of questioning myself, I press Allison. "Is there something you know about Dale and Eleanor?"

Allison shakes her head, looking apologetic. "There's only one thing I can tell you: Dale wants to get off the ship as soon as possible. And I think it's because he wants to escape."

Chapter 20

I finally kick the blanket off my body, letting out a suppressed squeal—I can't go back to sleep now.

It's only half past three, but my mind buzzes like it's already eight in the morning. Not just any mind—my detective mind.

Allison's voice echoes in my head, sharing her thoughts about Dale's... guilt. That's the word.

To say Dale is acting 'different' means he's acting guilty.

But I can't wrap my head around it.

As I sit up abruptly, Rex looks up from his bed, tilting his head at me with curiosity. I mutter to him, "It's your fault I can't sleep."

I swing my legs over the side of the bed and head to the bathroom. Even as I sit on the toilet, my thoughts drift back to that conversation with Allison—buzzing in my ear like a persistent mosquito.

After I flush, I step out of the bathroom and scan the room. There must be something I can do to quiet my racing thoughts. Like... investigate. Yes, it sounds counterintuitive, but the only way to calm my mind is to... solve our case.

This means I need to convince myself that Dale had nothing to do with Eleanor's death.

Giving up on a few hours of sleep, I shuffle to my small study table and power up my laptop. I just have to look into Dale one more time.

Finding Dale Bridges online is a breeze.

For someone who's new to the business world, I had no idea he owned a string of unique lodgings and homestays across Europe—like glass treehouses, picturesque underground bunkers, and modern greenhouse-style homes.

He graduated with a degree in business management and even earned an international MBA. So, even without Eleanor's support, he's doing quite well for himself.

Is his success a product of nepotism? Who knows?

Further digging reveals that Eleanor's husband passed away four years ago and that she has two daughters.

Dale's mother, Tamara Bridges, is a charity-loving, dog-rescuing woman who devotes her life to finding the perfect wine. If she's not making it herself in her San Polo vineyard—the same vineyard she won in her recent divorce settlement from Dale's father—then she's tasting others.

Dale's father is a celebrated pastry chef in Italy and throughout Europe.

Dale has a half-sister from his father, but nothing that connects to this murder case.

On the other hand, Dale's aunt, Mary Lowe Bridges-Hudson, leads a quiet life, devoid of controversial divorces or vineyard settlements. Instead, she runs a resort in The Azores with her family of four. I can see from her social media that she rarely visits Europe, except for New Year's.

Soon enough, I find myself scrolling through Dale's social media.

The first photo that catches my eye is of Eleanor, standing by the window in their suite on The Midnight Tide.

There's no caption, no context, but I understand its weight.

My chest constricts at the sight.

Setting my emotions aside, I search for a clue—anything that might point an accusing finger at Dale, against my better judgment.

I learn that Dale is quite the adrenaline junkie. From riding submarines to skydiving, he seems to have tried it all. He also has more posts featuring his grandmother than his mother.

Just a few months ago, he posted a candid photo of him hugging his laughing grandmother, captioned: "Thankful for all the women in my life, especially you, Gran. Happy birthday!"

On Mother's Day, he shared a picture of Eleanor and Tamara, captioned: "Generations of raising children with love."

I scroll further, noting that Dale never misses an opportunity to post birthday tributes for Eleanor. Even through the screen, it's clear how much he loves her.

But heartfelt posts don't automatically make Dale innocent, do they?

Any psychopath can post such sentiments and still commit murder.

I recall a documentary I watched where a husband wept on national television, begging for help to find his missing family—after he'd killed them.

Still, I'm struggling to see Dale as a murderer.

Where could he even get maitotoxin?

Where can anyone acquire it?

This time, I type "Where to get maitotoxin?" into my search bar, and the internet disappoints yet again. Aside from scientific jargon, I only learn that it's a toxin derived from a fish called 'maito,' first discovered in Tahiti.

Of course, there are no local stores selling it—it's not like arsenic or pesticide.

Reading and rereading the information, I can only conclude that the killer must have purposely extracted the poison from the fish and transferred it to the shellfish—just like we saw on camera the night Eleanor died.

This murder was premeditated from the start; I've known that.

But by Dale?

Still, Allison's words crawl under my skin, making me itch to find answers.

I can still remember her urging us to ease up on Dale; I recall her asking us to give him a break. So why the sudden shift?

Did Dale do something to her?

Or did Allison do something…?

The thought sends chills down my spine, prickling my arms.

Considering everyone a suspect, Allison is no exception. But why would it be her? I doubt she has any connection to Eleanor—apart from the fact that Eleanor adored her, as Ben mentioned when I first met Allison.

With this heavy thought weighing on my mind, I decide it's time to dig into Allison's background.

Like Dale, she's active on social media. Apart from a few stunning photos of herself at parties, on the beach, and even back on The Midnight Tide in her chef's uniform, she mostly shares pictures of her culinary creations.

Apparently, Allison has a food blog where she documents easy-to-cook meals with a gourmet flair.

She boasts a few thousand followers, too.

Other than a photo from a year ago in the lobby of the Emerald Hotel in London, I can't find any significant link to Eleanor.

So, I keep searching for "Allison Rye, Eleanor Bridges." Of course, I find about 400,000 related searches, but none of them are pertinent.

After spending hours trying to uncover a connection, dawn begins to break, and I find nothing.

Eventually, I prepare to start another day as the cruise director of the Midnight Tide. But I refuse to let Allison slip from scrutiny.

Maybe a more thorough background check will yield something useful; I'll have to add Allison to my growing list of suspects.

Whether Ben will be upset to learn I'm now considering Allison is a concern I'll tackle later.

After showering and getting dressed, my first priority is to visit Kelsey in the clinic at exactly eight in the morning.

"Good morning, Miss Dela Cruz! Can I help you?" a young doctor greets me as I enter.

I glance at Kelsey's bed, her body turned away as she sleeps. I decide not to disturb her, so I ask the doctor, "How's Kelsey Cho? Is she doing well?"

The doctor smiles. "Well, isn't she popular? But yeah, she's doing great. As soon as she feels completely better, we can give her a clean bill of health."

Her first statement catches me off guard. "What—what do you mean she's 'popular?'"

"Oh, nothing. It's just that you're the second person this morning to check up on her."

"Who's the other one, if I may ask? Is it the captain? The head of security, maybe?"

"Oh no. It's a woman—tall, blonde, pretty."

Allison? Not wanting to jump to conclusions, I quickly pull up Allison's social media page on my phone and show it to the doctor. "You mean her?"

She nods confidently. "Yep, that's the one."

What on earth was Allison doing here? How did she know Kelsey was in the clinic? More importantly, does she have anything to do with Eleanor's murder?

Chapter 21

It can't be right. It can't be Allison.

This seemingly sweet girl, with her genuine smiles and kind heart on this ship... or is that just the facade she's been presenting? Did those same smiles mask the emptiness in her eyes? Did her kindness mislead me from her true intentions?

But this isn't the time for wondering.

If I'm right, Allison is about to get away with murder; it's been three minutes since we docked at the port of Lerwick.

If I'm right, we completely overlooked Allison as a suspect. Now, as I reevaluate everything, I see her in a different light—as the perfect murderer.

Allison has been a chef for decades. Obtaining maito and extracting its poison would be a breeze for her. She's a former head chef of the Midnight Tide, so she knows exactly where all the cameras are located and which hallways lack surveillance.

Allison knows the kitchen staff—like Kelsey Cho. She's worked here long enough to know that the girls in Kelsey's cabin rarely lock their doors. Allison could've easily stolen the uniform and poisoned Kelsey to frame her for murder.

She even distracted Dale almost immediately after serving dinner, running off to hide the uniform and change into her evening attire.

Keeping Dale close allowed her to monitor the investigation's progress. And last night, when she realized her plan to kill Kelsey had failed, she must have decided to pin the blame on someone else. So she blames Dale.

It's all coming together.

The missing piece has been staring me in the face all along.

A wave of nausea washes over me at the thought that someone deceived me right in front of my eyes.

And it's the worst possible time to have left my radio behind. It's also the worst possible time for Ben to be ignoring my calls.

Come on, Ben. I silently urge him to pick up my fourth call in under two minutes.

As I do so, I speed-walk toward Allison's suite, which is much closer than the bridge.

I can update Ben later.

I need all the help I can get, so this time, I call Cole.

After three rings, he finally answers. "Good morning, Rose. I just called my colleague to help us out—"

I cut him off. "Cole, where are you? I need you and the others to alert security to watch all the exits of the ship. We can't let Allison Rye get off."

"What?" Cole sounds surprised and confused. "What do you mean?"

"Allison Rye," I repeat, urgency lacing my words. "She's a passenger on the ship—Ben's guest. You need to make sure she doesn't leave."

"Okay, but can you at least tell me why?"

"Because—" I arrive at one of the common lounges where a few passengers are gathered, making it tricky to explain that I suspect Allison killed Eleanor. I pause. "I'll tell you everything later. First, we need to find Allison and keep her on the ship."

"Alright, I'll give the order now."

"Thank you. I'm on my way to her suite."

"Okay then. Good luck."

I still have two decks to navigate to reach Allison's suite, so I sprint, taking the stairs two steps at a time.

Some passengers glance at me curiously as I speed past, but I ignore them until I find myself in front of Allison's door.

I knock three times at first.

When there's no answer, I knock five times, louder this time. Still nothing.

Crap... is Allison already gone?

Just as I'm about to knock again—hard enough to break the door—I hear a voice approaching. "Rose!"

I turn to see Ben jogging toward me. "Cole radioed me, so I came over as quickly as I could. Thankfully, I was just upstairs. What's going on?"

Pressed for time, I don't explain. "Do you have your master key with you? I need you to open this door."

Ben looks up at the room number and realizes whose room it is. "What's wrong? Is something wrong with Allison?"

"I'll explain later," I reply urgently. "Just please open the door. Now."

Seeing my agitation, Ben quickly checks his pockets, looking for the master keycard. He finds it and hands it to me.

I press the card against the door's reader, and within a second, the door beeps, indicating it's now unlocked.

I return the card to Ben, twist the doorknob, and push the door open.

The last time I was in here, the room was a slight mess. This time, it's pristine—clean and untouched. Even the bed is made, as if no one has slept there.

Is she gone? A wave of dread rises in my throat.

Quickly, I cross the room and fling open the bathroom door; the sink is half-empty. But it's devoid of any of Allison's belongings.

She isn't in the shower either.

I dash out of the room, frantically, perhaps looking like a maniac to Ben, but I can't afford to care.

I stop before the closet, praying that Allison's clothes remain. When I swing the cabinet doors open, it's empty.

Ben, standing behind me, sees the vacant cabinet, too. "What the hell's happening, Rose?"

I glance at the open door, ensuring no one can hear me. "Allison did it. She killed Eleanor."

"What?" Ben's face pales immediately. "How—how did that even happen?"

I shake my head, the details still swirling in my mind. "I don't know. Last night, I ran into her around two in the morning; she said she went out for a smoke. Then—"

"Smoke?" Ben interrupts. "Allison doesn't smoke."

"That's what I thought." I shoot Ben an apologetic look. "That means she lied about why she was outside last night. I think she was getting rid of evidence."

"The phone?"

"It would make sense if she did; we called her through that phone last night."

"But we don't know for sure..."

I understand Ben's hesitation; Allison wasn't just the Midnight Tide's head chef—she's also Ben's friend.

So, I add, "Allison visited Kelsey in the clinic earlier today."

Ben's expression grows grim. "What do you mean? How would she know? We didn't tell anyone about it."

"Exactly. But she somehow knew—as if she figured out Kelsey would either be sick or... dead."

"This is ridiculous," Ben mutters mostly to himself. "Why would she even do something like that?"

I pause, realizing I have no clear answers.

In murder cases, motive is crucial. So why did Allison do it? I have to know. We have to know. And there's only one person who could give us the answer... except she has vanished from the ship.

Chapter 22

"Did you find her?" I ask Cole as I meet him at one of the vessel's passenger exits.

Cole shakes his head, frustration etched across his features. "No. I have my men searching for her everywhere on the ship."

Ben chimes in, "How about Dale's suite?"

"We already checked," Cole replies. "She's not there."

The dreadful thought that Allison could've actually escaped makes my heart drop to my stomach. "Do you think she's already... left?"

The three of us exchange horrified looks, none of us daring to voice the fear hanging in the air.

Just then, Stacy arrives, breathless. "Sorry to be ceremoniously late for the party... whatever it is."

She immediately sees through our grim expressions. "Did something happen?"

I nod at her, lowering my voice to a whisper. "We found the killer."

Stacy gasps, her hand flying to her mouth as if to stifle the gravity of our conversation. "Oh god. Who is it?"

"Allison Rye," I reply, my words leaving a bitter taste on my tongue.

"Well, where is she?"

"We couldn't find her on the ship," I admit, frustration boiling within me for not trusting my instincts last night. "I'm worried she's already slipped away."

Stacy glances at her designer watch. "It's only been ten minutes since the ship docked. We might still catch her."

My eyebrows knit together. "You think we can just run after her?"

"Only if we leave now," she insists, her confidence a much-needed balm to my anxiety. Then she looks at me expectantly. "Come on, Rose. You have enough experience as a private investigator to know what Allison would do next."

Hearing the certainty in Stacy's voice helps to calm my racing thoughts.

She's right. I do have experience in investigations, and I can't let panic cloud my judgment. "Allison is going to try to escape the city, so we need to ask the police to set up roadblocks. We have to make sure she can't get away."

Cole quickly pulls out his phone and starts dialing. "I'll call the police now."

Out of the corner of my eye, I see Ben nodding. "Let's discuss this as we look for her. Come on."

The four of us hurry down the vessel, and I continue speaking. "Once Allison realizes there are police checkpoints, the first thing she'll do is hide. She'll look for a discreet place to wait this out until it blows over."

We finally step off the vessel, the sun's rays hitting our faces like a warm welcome.

I add, "We're talking about inns and motels. Any place that requires identification is the least likely spot for her."

Ben mutters to himself, "So, no five-star hotels. Got it."

"Does she know anyone in Lerwick?" I ask.

"Um, I'm not sure. In the few years we worked together, I never heard her mention any acquaintances here," Ben responds.

"Okay, good," I continue. "She's likely anticipating her cards being tracked, so from here on out, she'll probably use cash. We need to check all the banks and ATMs."

"Anything else?" Ben asks, jotting down mental notes.

I take a moment to think. "For now, that's all I can come up with."

Just then, Cole returns. "I've notified the police. I also sent them a photo of Allison."

"Great," I say, feeling the tightness in my throat ease slightly, though it lingers. "Now, we just need to find Allison in the city."

Ben speaks decisively. "Cole and I will hit the banks and ATMs. You and your sister should check the motels and inns. Let's meet back here."

I nod and turn to Stacy. "Let's go."

Stacy and I decide it's too time-consuming to switch taxis constantly. Renting a car would take half an hour, so we hire a cab driver for the day at a hefty price.

The cab driver seems to be on our side, ready to help us scour the city.

Surprisingly, there are numerous motels and inns here. Excluding anything above a three-star rating still leaves us with over thirty options.

We better hurry.

While heading to the nearest motel, Stacy and I take turns calling every other hotel on our list, asking if they have a guest named Allison Rye. We instruct them to contact us if she shows up.

Naturally, they bombard us with questions. Some refuse to disclose guest information, as they should.

I concoct a foolproof excuse: Allison left her bag on the Midnight Tide and hasn't realized it's missing.

That simple line often gets them to inform us that Allison isn't there.

Upon arriving at the first motel, Stacy and I leap out of the cab, repeating our cover story about Allison's bag.

This one responds quickly; it's not complicated. Perhaps it's the rundown Bayside motel that hasn't seen much upkeep.

I can see mold creeping along the ceiling as we speak.

When we learn that Allison isn't there, we move on to the next inn. Again, we call other motels from the cab.

This method proves efficient; within an hour, we've visited four motels and called twelve others.

Ben calls me to update us—they haven't found anything yet and are waiting for police assistance to ease the inquiries at the banks.

With no arrest warrants, we have to play it smart.

But as smart as we are, the second hour ticks by, and I can't shake the feeling that Allison is one step ahead of us.

What are the odds that she had thought this through? Could that be why she was so restless last night? Was she plotting the perfect escape?

I try not to dwell on it.

Once we finish the motels on our list, I decide to check the hospitals, just in case Allison ends up there... for any reason.

If we can't nail her down today, we'll need hard evidence to convince a judge to issue a wanted list. Perhaps even broadcast it across Europe's national channels to speed up the search.

Feeling disheartened, guilty, and anxious, Stacy and I have no choice but to head back to the Midnight Tide.

As we approach the port, police checkpoints are set up.

At least we have the cops on our side in this literal manhunt.

I can't help but think that Cole must have pulled some strings to get the police mobilized for this search, even without concrete evidence... yet.

I cling to optimism—we have to find something on Allison soon. I need to believe that.

Arriving at the port, the Midnight Tide looms just a few meters away. Stacy offers to pay for the expensive cab ride.

Normally, I'd argue with her, but I'm too anxious to care. All I want is to find Allison.

Back at our rendezvous point, I don't see Ben or Cole yet. I glance at my phone; Ben has left me a message saying they'll arrive in twenty minutes.

I can't waste twenty minutes standing in the sun.

"Can you wait for them here?" I ask Stacy. "Tell them I'm going back inside the ship to look for Allison again. She might have known we were coming, so she could be hiding onboard."

I'm not even sure if I'm making sense, but she has to be somewhere, right?

She can't possibly have jet-skied away to another city, can she? There's no hidden trapdoor on this ship—wait, is there?

Allison knows this vessel better than I do.

With that thought gnawing at me, I don't wait for Stacy to respond; I start sprinting up the gangway of the grand vessel.

Maybe she's hiding in the kitchen; she would know that place like the back of her hand, wouldn't she?

But as I make my way to the kitchen, a male voice calls out, "Rose!"

I turn, expecting either Ben or Cole. Instead, it's Dale, sporting an ice pack against his cheek like someone just clocked him.

"Dale," I say, meeting him halfway. "What happened to your face? Are you okay?"

"Y-yeah," he replies, seeming distracted and wincing slightly as he presses the ice pack to his skin. "But I've been looking for you and Captain Anderson all morning."

I honestly don't have time for small talk with Dale right now, even if he seems to be in a better mood than usual.

Still, I put on my best cruise director smile. "Well, now I'm here. What's this about?"

Dale glances around, his expression shifting as if he's about to share a secret. "I can't really tell you anything here, but I can show you."

I blink at him, curiosity piquing. "Can you at least give me a hint? I'm in the middle of something very important—"

"It's about Allison," Dale speaks urgently. "I can take you to her right now."

Chapter 23

Before leading me to where Allison is, Dale decides to explain the chaos in his suite.

And I mean chaos—pillows strewn across the floor, the carpet oddly rolled to one side, a shattered vase, and a heavy armchair tipped over as if a fight broke out.

It looks like someone ransacked the place.

Dale begins, "Allison and I may have gotten into a bit of a scuffle, which explains the black eye coming in on my face."

Mortified, I scan the room before turning back to him. "What happened? And where is she?"

"I... may have locked her in the bathroom." Dale bats his eyelashes, feigning innocence. "But I did it for the same reason you're looking for her."

I suppress a gasp. "How—how did you know?"

"I overheard you talking as you were leaving the vessel," he admits. "But let me explain."

Dale walks over to the toppled armchair and rights it, clapping the top as if it were a trophy. "Um, have a seat...?"

Still reeling from the mess, I decide I'm safer on my feet. "No, thank you. I'll stand."

"Understandable," Dale replies, taking a seat in the chair he offered. "To cut to the chase since I know you want to see Allison, she came to me earlier this morning, saying you and Ben might try to frame us for my grandmother's murder."

The way Dale looks at me could feel threatening—until his eyes soften, and he chuckles nervously. "I guess you can see why I believed her; you and Ben haven't exactly been on my side. And I understand that."

I feel a pang of sympathy for him all over again.

In doing my job, I had to consider Dale as a suspect. It's what they call an 'occupational hazard,' but that doesn't make it any easier.

I breathe deeply. "I'm so sorry, Dale."

"No, don't be. You were just doing your job." He offers me a small smile. "But I didn't realize it sooner; Allison has been feeding me so many lies that I actually believed her when she said that. So, I hid her here in my suite this morning."

Dale's regret is palpable as he continues. "She asked me to... escape with her. But before we could do that, I needed to make sure none of you knew what we were up to. So, I told her I'd be her lookout, but I really intended to confront you and Captain Anderson."

I nod, listening intently.

Dale continues, "That's when I saw you, the captain, and the head of security speaking by the ship's exit. It looked serious, so I thought I'd eavesdrop. That's when I heard you thought Allison did it—not in a 'framing' way."

Now feels like the right time to tell Dale the truth. "Because we weren't framing anyone. Not you or Allison. We can't frame her because... she did it."

I say those words with unwavering confidence; I know now that we're on the right track.

Dale nods as he reaches into his jacket pocket, pulling out a rolled-up tissue. He carefully unravels it to reveal a small glass bottle.

"I believe you," he says, placing the bottle on the coffee table.

My eyes widen at the sight of it—just half an inch tall, perfect for containing a lethal dose of poison. "Is this...?"

"From Allison? Yes. When I confronted her about my grandmother's murder, let's just say she went berserk. Hence the scuffle. While I was trying to get her off me, she dropped this. Her reaction told me everything I needed to know. If we send it to a forensic lab, I'm betting we'll find the same poison that killed my grandma."

I can't believe the perfect evidence is sitting right in front of me.

Thankfully, Dale has the foresight not to smear his fingerprints all over it.

Feeling a wave of relief wash over me, I sense the weight of the world lifting from my shoulders. "Thanks for this, Dale."

"No, thank you," Dale replies, standing up from the chair. "Now, do you want to go see Allison? I have to warn you; I had to 'disable' her to keep her from getting too violent."

I'm not sure what he means by 'disable,' but I nod, determined to see for myself.

Dale leads me to the bathroom, where I finally understand what 'disable' means—Allison is cuffed to the shower's safety railing, a cloth wrapped around her mouth.

As soon as she sees me, she hums a muffled protest behind the curtain and tugs on the cuffs with her arm.

Dale leans closer and whispers, "Don't ask me where I got the cuffs."

I let out a wry chuckle. "I wasn't going to."

With that, Dale steps away from the shower area, handing me a small key for the cuffs. "All yours, Miss Dela Cruz."

As I hear Dale's footsteps retreat into the other room, I walk inside the shower area, where Allison's muffled protests grow louder.

The first thing I do is untie the cloth around her mouth.

"Allison immediately spews frantically. "I don't know what's happening! Thank God you're here! I think Dale is trying to frame me for his grandmother's murder!"

Is she really using the same lie she told Dale?

Looking into her suddenly teary eyes, I crouch down to speak at her level. "Allison, I'll give you a chance to redeem yourself—maybe mitigate your crime a little. I won't turn you over to the cops yet, but I'll hold you in the ship's cell. If you confess and show remorse, I'll put in a good word with the police. How about that?"

Allison's fearful eyes quickly turn to annoyance. Smirking, she scoffs. "What the hell do you think you're doing?"

I don't break my gaze from her piercing stare. "Arresting you."

Ben, Cole, and I, along with the police, agree to hold Allison in the ship's cell for 24 hours. We're all hoping that keeping her here will make her confession easier.

After all, she should feel less intimidated in the Midnight Tide's custody.

In the meantime, we've turned over the little but incriminating evidence we have against Allison Rye—that was three hours ago.

Once the glass bottle's analysis confirms traces of maitotoxin, the police will issue an arrest warrant for her.

So, if we want her to talk sooner, we need to interrogate her.

Ben is the first to head inside the jail cell to talk to Allison. He insists she still needs a friend during this difficult time.

I'd shut down his sympathy if I didn't know he genuinely cares for Allison as a friend. So, I let him be.

We ask him to record his conversation with Allison if she confesses to him.

Cole and I wait outside.

About 40 minutes later, Ben exits the cell with a sad look on his face, shaking his head at us.

In a quiet voice, he informs us, "Allison maintains she's innocent and that Dale is framing her."

But Dale has already volunteered to give his formal statement to the police—something the actual killer wouldn't easily do.

I sigh. "Well, we have to get her to confess. We owe Dale that much."

I don't tell Ben or Cole, but I'm worried Allison may still get away with murder if we don't uncover her motive.

It wouldn't make sense for someone to target another like that randomly.

The crime is too personal. And without Allison's motive, she's as good as a stranger to Eleanor.

So we have to find out before Dale really becomes a suspect.

Cole speaks up. "Can I try talking to her?"

If Cole can talk a man out of jumping off a cargo vessel, he can probably talk some sense into Allison.

I glance at Ben, who looks like he's thinking the same thing.

So, I nod at Cole. "Go ahead, Cole. We'll wait out here for you."

As Cole heads inside, I turn to Ben. "Are you okay?"

Ben gives me a small smile that doesn't quite reach his eyes. "I'm alright. Don't worry about me."

A part of me wants to pull him into a comforting embrace; I can only imagine how difficult this is for a friend.

An hour passes before Cole finally comes out of the cell.

Judging by how long it took him to return, I feel a glimmer of hope.

"So?" I blink at Cole with anticipation.

Cole shakes his head. "I didn't think she'd be that... difficult. She barely talked, and when she did, she said a lot of rude things."

I tap Cole's arm. "Thanks for trying."

Ben asks, "Rose, should you give it a shot?"

"Not yet," I reply. "I think we should give her some time to reflect."

If there's one thing I know about breaking criminals, it's that a little time can give them enough to ponder their choices.

Maybe in the silence of her loneliness, she'll hear her conscience speaking.

For now, we leave her be.

I leave her alone until dinnertime rolls around, and I need to bring her a meal.

It's been eight hours since we locked her up.

I hope that's enough time to get Allison talking.

As I arrive with a tray of hot meals, I find Allison pacing in circles. "Hey, Allison."

She turns to face me, her expression filled with disgust. "You won't hear what you want me to say."

I slide the food towards her. "The only thing I want to hear from you is the truth."

"The truth is, I'm being framed for murder. But none of you believe me."

"We both know that's not the truth, Allison."

"How do you know?" she challenges, her defiance rising.

Since we've received the lab results from the police, I have more ammunition to pressure her.

Thankfully, I bring a printed copy with me. I show it to Allison. "We've identified the poison you used and found the same toxin in the glass bottle Dale got from you."

Allison doesn't even glance at the paper. "How do you know Dale didn't bring it on the ship and plant it on me?"

"Allison, there's no need to drag this out. We know you did it."

"Apart from that piece of paper, what other evidence do you have?"

I sense she's fishing for evidence—trying to find a way to discredit it. So, I don't give her anything.

Instead, I ask, "Why did you do it, Allison?"

She plays the fool. "Do what?"

"Kill Eleanor."

"I didn't."

If Allison thinks she can wear me down, she's mistaken. I can stay here all night if it means getting something out of her.

I grab a nearby chair and position it right in front of the jail cell.

Allison watches me curiously as I sit comfortably. "What are you doing?"

"Waiting for you to talk."

"Then you'll be here for a while."

"That's alright," I say, crossing my legs as I scroll through my phone.

Allison scoffs but eventually sits back down on her cot.

For the next few minutes, it's quiet between us.

Allison mindlessly jabs her food with a fork while I pretend to be engrossed in my phone.

It's uncomfortable, but the fact that Allison keeps glancing at me tells me my presence is bothering her more than hers is bothering me.

Fifteen minutes in, Allison finally speaks. "What makes you think you'll get through to me?"

"I don't," I reply nonchalantly, not looking at her. "I just know you had a reason. And I want to understand it."

"Let's say I killed her, hypothetically; why should I tell you why?"

"Because if you don't, you'll have to explain to people who don't care about your feelings."

"And you care?"

"More than those detectives outside, yes." I finally meet Allison's gaze. "I know you had a reason for doing it, and I'm not judging you for it. But I can make this easier for you. All you have to do is tell me why you did it."

Allison doesn't answer right away. Instead, she studies me, perhaps with sadness reflecting in her eyes. "I don't trust you."

"You don't have to. But once you go out there and the police take you in, they'll be ruthless."

Allison considers this for a moment, and then the most heartbreaking cry escapes her lips. Her voice cracks as she wails, desperately trying to catch her breath.

She cries like a child behind those metal bars.

I let her be—I think she needs to let it all out.

After a moment, Allison collects herself, wiping tears and snot from her face. She finally nods. "Shouldn't you be recording this?"

Epilogue
Eight days after catching the killer

Allison Rye is hurt to the point where she believes that murder is the answer to her pain—that's what I learned from our conversation a week ago.

The memory of our talk lingers in my mind like a haunting tune I can't turn off, no matter how hard I try.

I can't help but feel a sense of pity for her.

Eleanor blindsided her, and in a desperate act, Allison poisoned her in return. Talk about twisted retribution.

"She found me on the Midnight Tide and offered me a once-in-a-lifetime opportunity to work at her London hotel as her executive chef." I can still hear Allison's words echoing in my head, her tear-streaked face vivid in my memory. "She scouted me, saying that a talent like mine shouldn't be hidden away."

The way her voice cracks at nearly every syllable constricts my heart even now, a week later. "She told me to resign from the Midnight Tide as soon as the cruise ended, and that a job would be waiting for me."

And Allison did just that—she resigned and asked Eleanor for one week to move from Amsterdam to London.

So, she canceled her apartment lease, even paying a hefty fine to do so, and opened a new one in London with her savings. She bought new furniture and appliances for her loft in the bustling UK city.

Believing she was on the brink of a better job, Allison splurged a little on her family and friends.

After all, Eleanor had given her an irresistible offer, so Allison felt like she had just hit the employment jackpot—spending a bit too much wouldn't hurt, would it?

Swiping her cards felt like no big deal.

But when Allison arrived at the Emerald Hotel in London for her supposed first day, she was devastated to learn that another chef had already filled the position just a day earlier.

"I begged to speak with Eleanor Bridges," she told me. "I explained that Eleanor scouted me personally, but the London branch said they had no record of it. At that point, I had no contract to protect me, just a few text messages between Eleanor and me. By then, she wasn't responding or picking up."

Eleanor practically kicked her to the curb and left her... for dead.

For weeks, Allison tried to contact Eleanor, but to no avail. At one point, the police were called because she refused to leave the hotel lobby and caused a scene.

None of those incidents were documented, so we couldn't uncover them even with the help of a private investigator.

And because she made such a ruckus, rumors of a crazy ex-chef spread through London's culinary circles.

She had quite the reputation there.

Since Allison had already paid for her London lease, she managed to stay there for the next two months, trying to

find work at other five-star hotels and high-end restau-
rants. Still, due to the nasty rumors, she couldn't secure a
position.

In those two months, she ended up taking a sous chef
job at a quirky Italian restaurant that barely paid her half
of what she used to earn on the Midnight Tide.

Devastated and depressed doesn't even begin to cover
how she felt.

She was deep in debt, on the verge of being broke, an
angry woman who had it all—only to lose everything due
to an empty promise.

In just one week, she gave up her stable job and moved
to a new city, only to watch it all slip away.

On her last day in her London apartment, she attempted
to take her own life.

Strangely, she was sent to a psychiatric ward, where the
first thoughts of killing Eleanor haunted her each night for
the next two weeks.

From that point forward, she became obsessed with the
idea of murder.

Six months after quitting her job on the Midnight Tide,
Allison started a blog that somehow began making her
money... somehow.

It was just enough to cover some of her debts, not nearly
enough to restart her life.

She had to give up the luxurious lifestyle she had known
and moved in with her sister, lying about how well the blog
was doing and claiming she no longer needed to work a
nine-to-five.

By the ninth month, she almost forgot about her
vendetta.

That is until she unexpectedly ran into Eleanor at a
high-end restaurant her friend invited her to.

Allison felt that rage bubble up again—but instead of killing Eleanor, she wanted to confront her. Maybe humiliate her.

But when she approached Eleanor, the wealthy woman didn't even recognize her.

Eleanor even mistook Allison for a waitress.

Humiliated, Allison returned to that dark place in her mind. For three months, she plotted Eleanor's death.

Fortune smiled on her when Ben called, inviting her to join the very first "Dutchman Cruise" of the Midnight Tide.

Allison knew Eleanor wouldn't miss a chance to sail with her favorite cruise line. So, she arrived at the vessel with poison in hand.

And she succeeded.

Recalling it now leaves a bitter taste in my mouth.

Drowning in melancholy, I'm jolted back to reality when I feel a tap on my shoulder. "Rose, disembarking the ship, huh?"

I blink, and suddenly I'm walking the familiar halls of the Midnight Tide, almost at the vessel's exit.

I look over my shoulder and see Ben strolling beside me in casual clothes—it's been a while since I've seen him out of his captain's uniform.

I adjust the strap of my small duffel bag. "Well, yes. I get one week off before the next cruise, right?"

"Yeah," Ben smiles. "I'd offer you more days if I didn't need you back on my ship."

"I barely did my job as a cruise director."

"Well, I can't blame you. You were busy solving a murder."

The smile on my face fades slowly at the mention of 'murder.' It brings Allison back to mind. "How is... Allison, by the way?"

Ben mirrors my expression, his gaze distant and lips pressed into a thin line. "She confessed to everything. Thanks to you. Her first hearing is next week."

I nod. "Well, I hope her sentence gets reduced."

"I hope so too," Ben agrees. "Oh, and I heard Eleanor's family is having a private funeral at the Bridges' estate in London."

"Dale got an earful, I presume?"

"From what he told me last, his family wishes he'd said something sooner. So, yes."

Ben and I walk off the platform connected to the ship.

Outside, the afternoon light is a vibrant mix of pink and orange—the sunset closing in on us as we gather our things.

Suddenly, I hear a car honking.

Looking over to the parking lot, across the crisscross fence, I see Stacy waving her arms at me. I turn to Ben. "That's my ride; I better get going. See you next week?"

"Sure," Ben says, flashing me another of his boyish smiles. "See you then."

As I take my first step toward the parking lot, Ben calls out to me. "Rose, hold on."

I turn back again. "Yes, Captain?"

Ben inhales sharply and exhales as if he's nervous. Then he speaks. "I was wondering if you'd... like to grab dinner sometime?"

"Sure," I say, trying to keep my tone casual. "I'll make sure to call Cole—"

"N-no," Ben interjects. "I mean, it's not that I don't want Cole and your sister to join us. It's just that... how do I put this?"

He looks like a kid who doesn't know what to do, glancing around and scratching his neck in uncertainty. He stutters as he adds, "I'm thinking we... you and I... we should... um..."

Seeing his face turn a shade that rivals the sunset, I realize what he's trying to say.

Unable to contain my laughter, I finish his sentence, hoping I'm not misreading the situation. "Go on a date?"

Ben's eyes widen.

He nods, looking both surprised and relieved. "Y-yeah. We should... go on a date."

"Okay," I reply flatly, even though my insides are dancing with excitement. "How does Wednesday sound?"

Ben chuckles. "That sounds amazing."

I smile at him, my cheeks flushing with warmth. "I'll see you then."

Unlock the next chapter:

Visit – https://www.amazon.com/dp/B0DPNH749Y
(Piercing Shadows Book 2)

The mystery doesn't end with *Dead Man's Dish*—it's only just begun. In ***Piercing Shadows***, Rose Dela Cruz is drawn into a case unlike any she's faced before. The deeper she digs, the more unsettling the truths become.

Read the next book in the series to step back into the tension, the twists, and the relentless pursuit of the truth. Get ready for a journey that will leave you breathless. The search for answers is far from over.

Sneak Peek

The Midnight Tide promises glamour, luxury, and an escape from reality—until the lights go out, and murder steps aboard.

As cruise director of the Midnight Tide, Rose Dela Cruz is used to handling just about anything—extravagant parties, difficult passengers, even the occasional stormy sea. But when an unexpected blackout plunges the luxurious ship into darkness, Rose knows something is very wrong.

Moments later, a ringing phone shatters the uneasy silence. Meadow Dunn, a social media celebrity adored by millions, has been found dead in her suite. Now, Rose must unravel a twisted mystery, surrounded by hundreds of frightened passengers and a growing list of suspects—all trapped together at sea.

With Rex, her loyal and intuitive beagle, sniffing for clues, and Cole Hester, Head of Security, working tirelessly by her side, Rose peels back layers of deceit hidden behind picture-perfect smiles. But Meadow's glamorous circle of friends seems oddly unaffected by tragedy, making Rose wonder if envy is the real motive—or if something even darker lurks behind their pretty faces.

As the Midnight Tide nears its next port, time ticks mercilessly forward. Rose must catch a killer determined to vanish into the crowd, or risk letting them slip away forever. The closer she comes to the truth, the more dangerous the investigation becomes. Can Rose unmask the killer before the ship docks, or will the shadows swallow the truth for good?

Piercing Shadows delivers a heart-racing, addictive mystery full of charming characters, sharp wit, and the kind of twisty secrets you can't wait to unravel.

<u>***Unlock the next chapter***</u>:
Visit – https://www.amazon.com/dp/B0DPNH749Y
<u>*(Piercing Shadows Book 2)*</u>
Prologue
Night of the Incident

Ring. Ring. Ring.
Nothing shatters the silence more than a phone piercing through it just moments after the lights flicker back to life on The Midnight Tide. The number is unknown, and an unsettling instinct stirs deep within me.

The ship hums as power surges back through its veins, yet the electric tension lingers, heavy in the air. Waves pound against the hull, their rhythm muffled beneath the familiar melody streaming through the speakers. I should feel reassured, but that sense of safety remains just out of reach.

The three minutes of darkness cling to my thoughts, raw and vivid, the afterimage of emergency lights still etched in my mind. But this phone call sends my pulse skittering again. Whoever it is has timed their call perfectly, as if they've been watching, waiting for the moment my heartbeat begins to calm.

I answer, striving to keep my voice steady. "Rose Dela Cruz speaking."

Beside me, Julia Hart, my new assistant, stands with her bright demeanor still intact, though a faint crease of worry lines her brow. I turn my gaze away, focusing on the trembling breaths coming from the other end of the line.

The voice—though shaking—is unmistakable, weighted with desperation and disbelief. "Miss Dela Cruz... hurry. It's my best friend. She's—she's dead."

Dead. The word crashes into me like a wave, an unwelcome echo of my past. I've trained myself to mask my reactions, yet that single word always lands like an unexpected blow, dredging up haunting memories. I've spent countless sleepless nights reliving the shadows of the last tragedy on this ship, fragments swirling in my mind—an empty dining hall, a sudden fall, an outstretched hand. And always, the bitter truth: I wasn't able to save them.

Is it a blessing or a curse that my history as a private investigator has led me here? Captain Anderson may not have hired me for my crime-solving skills, but that hasn't stopped me from employing them. And now, it's happening again.

"Miss Rose?" Julia's wide eyes reflect my uncertainty, but I force a small, practiced smile.

"I'll handle it, Julia. Why don't you take the rest of the evening off?"

Relief flickers across her face, though she tilts her head, not entirely convinced. "All right, then. I'll see you tomorrow!"

I nod, watching her retreat down the hallway. The moment she's out of sight, my smile fades, replaced by a gnawing sense of dread. My hand presses against the cool wall, grounding me as I gather my thoughts. Taking a steadying breath, I dial Captain Ben Anderson's number, a chill running down my spine at the thought of disturbing him with this news.

Ben answers instantly, his voice warm and comforting. "Rose, I was just about to call you."

For a brief moment, I consider letting him remain blissfully unaware of the storm brewing on this line. But I owe him the truth. "Captain, there's been an incident. I need you to come to Serena Hampton's suite with me. The same one we visited this morning."

The silence on the other end is telling; he understands more than I'm saying. "I'll call Cole. We'll meet you there as soon as possible."

Ending the call, I focus on keeping my steps steady as I navigate toward the upper-deck suites. My heart pounds, an eerie sense of anticipation building with each footfall.

When I reach the door of Suite 230, Ben and Cole Hester, the ship's head of security, are already waiting. Their expressions mirror my own—serious, tense. We share a look of silent resolve.

"Rose," Ben murmurs, searching my face. "Are you ready?"

The absurdity of his question almost makes me laugh. Are any of us truly ready for death? But I stifle my hesitation. "Let's go."

Cole's voice is barely a whisper as he murmurs, "I'll never get used to this."

I nod, reaching out to clap his shoulder. "Neither will I. None of us should."

Ben knocks softly, his body tense, his stance protective. Within moments, the door cracks open, revealing a tear-streaked face—a petite, dark-haired young woman, her eyes bloodshot and puffy. She steps aside, letting us in without a word.

We enter the muted glow of the suite's ambient lighting, our gazes sweeping over the living area. A blonde girl sits on the edge of the bed, her shoulders shaking with silent sobs. Serena Hampton, the caller, is nowhere to be seen. And from what I can gather, neither is Meadow Dunn.

"Where is she?" I ask, my voice low, half-hoping I'm mistaken.

The dark-haired girl lifts her arm, a trembling finger pointing toward the bathroom.

I steel myself, moving past the suite's main room, my gaze locked on the cracked-open door of the bathroom. The silence deepens with every step, an ominous weight settling in my stomach until I finally cross the threshold and take in the scene before me.

Two figures huddle on the bathroom floor. Serena Hampton sits against the cold tile, her raven hair tangled around her face, mascara streaked down her cheeks, and in her lap lies a body. Blood stains Serena's white shirt, spreading in an unmistakable pattern across her chest, and the girl sprawled across her lap—Meadow—is eerily still.

Serena lifts her tear-filled eyes to meet mine, and the raw desperation reflected there is unmistakable. "Please, help us. I think she's... I think she's gone."

A chill sweeps over me as I look down at Meadow, her lifeless face staring blankly at the ceiling. I try to avoid looking too closely at her once-vibrant green eyes, now fixed in a hollow gaze, but my instincts won't let me look away.

The wounds are impossible to miss. Blood mars her forehead, streaks running down from two small punctures above her left eyebrow and temple, leaving stark red trails across her cheek. Another wound, deep and raw, marks her throat, blood pooling around her collarbone.

"Cole," I say, my voice steady but strained. "Let's move her back so we can examine Meadow."

He nods, his hands gentle as he helps Serena settle Meadow's head onto the cold tile. She shudders but doesn't protest, rising to her feet as Cole guides her out of the room.

Taking a deep breath, I crouch beside Meadow, forcing myself to look beyond the blood. Something glints faintly from within the wounds. I narrow my eyes, leaning in just enough to make out the strange metallic shape embedded in her skin.

Nails. Metal nails.

My stomach twists, but I push the sensation down, steadying myself with another breath. Death may be familiar territory, but the brutal sight before me is something I doubt I'll ever be able to shake.

Chapter 1
Three Days Before the Incident

"I can sit this one out if you two want some time alone," my sister, Stacy Dela Cruz, says, leaning casually against the doorway with a smirk as she slips on her diamond-studded earrings. "I mean, this is your chance for a romantic night with the handsome Captain Anderson."

I scoff, adjusting the neckline of my black halter dress, trying not to laugh. "It's not a date, Stacy. For the hundredth time."

She squints at me, her gaze sweeping over my outfit, lingering on the thigh-high slit. "Right. You just happen to be dressed like it's date night at The Concertgebouw."

"It's an orchestra, Stacy," I reply, feigning exasperation as I run my hands over the smooth fabric. "And it's not exactly casual."

"Uh-huh," she hums, a knowing grin spreading across her face. "So you're saying you and Ben casually decided to spend my last night in Amsterdam indulging in a little classical music. Very low-key."

"It's a send-off," I insist, rolling my eyes as she flops down on my bed. "And Ben likes having you around, so yes, you're absolutely coming. Don't even think about escaping."

"He better like having me around," she laughs, shrugging on a silver shawl. "I'm practically his sister-in-law already."

"Stacy!" I gasp, my cheeks warming as I laugh at her outrageousness. "You're impossible."

"It's true!" She throws her hands up in mock surrender, her smile infectious. "I mean, you've been together for over a year now. If you're not ready to make it official, you never will be."

Her teasing strikes a chord, and I glance at her, the only one who truly knows my every thought, every secret. "We're taking things slow," I murmur, brushing invisible dust from my skirt to avoid her probing gaze.

"Slow?" she scoffs, hands on her hips. "More like snail-paced. You're practically going backward."

I throw my hands in the air, laughing in defeat. "Fine, I'm taking things slow, if you must know."

At that moment, Rex, my beagle, hops up beside me, nudging my arm with his soft head. He looks at Stacy with wide, expectant eyes, his tail wagging eagerly—always on alert, especially since I rescued him from a less-than-affectionate owner.

I ruffle his ears. "If only Rex could talk. He'd probably tell you how annoying you're being."

Rex, predictably, just thumps his tail, blissfully unaware of our banter.

Just then, my phone rings, the caller ID flashing Ben's name, and a flutter of excitement races through me, quickly masked by a casual demeanor as I answer. "Hey, Ben."

"I'm just outside your apartment," he says, his voice warm and familiar. "You two ready?"

I nod, fighting back a smile. "We'll be right down."

As I end the call, Stacy's eyebrows lift, her face lighting up in a mocking grin. "We'll be right down…"

"Out," I laugh, guiding her toward the door as she mimics my tone, dragging out the syllables. "Come on. If we're late, he'll blame me for holding up his precious schedule."

We ride down to the lobby, Rex watching us with quiet alertness, as if sensing I'm not ready to let this night end. Moments later, Ben's SUV pulls up, and, as always, he steps out to open the door.

"Les dames d'abord," he says, his brown eyes catching mine, a teasing smirk playing on his lips.

I feel a blush creeping up my cheeks, and my response comes automatically. "Oui, monsieur," I mutter with a smile, climbing into the passenger seat while Stacy slips into the back, her knowing grin barely contained.

Ben drives us through the glowing streets of Amsterdam, the canals reflecting the city lights in an ethereal glow. As The Concertgebouw comes into view, its grand arches and timeless elegance cast a spell over all of us.

Stepping inside, I'm struck by the grandeur, the vintage beauty of it all. Rich mahogany tones fill the hall, and golden lights cast warm, ambient shadows over the crowd settling into their seats. I steal a glance at Stacy, whose mouth is slightly open, visibly impressed.

"This place is unreal," she murmurs, her eyes wide with wonder.

"It is," I agree, sharing a smile with Ben, who seems pleased with himself for suggesting it.

Guiding us to our seats, Ben gently places his hand on my lower back, and a surge of warmth spreads through me, something deeper than just the ambiance. "Sorry for the third row. I tried to get us closer."

"Front-row seats are overrated," I say, laughing softly, feeling that familiar thrill whenever he's near.

Settling in between Stacy and Ben, I'm almost overwhelmed by the intimacy of the space, how the world narrows down to just the three of us. After a few moments of anticipation, the orchestra begins its first movement, filling the hall with Beethoven's Symphony No. 5. It's stirring and breathtaking, each note reaching out and wrapping itself around us.

By the end of the performance, we're on our feet, joining the crowd in an unspoken agreement that this deserves a standing ovation. Even Stacy is howling in her own way, clapping with enthusiasm.

"That was incredible," she gushes as we make our way out, her energy infectious. "I'm so glad I didn't sit this one out."

"Were you planning to?" Ben arches a brow, a smirk dancing on his lips.

She glances at me with a mischievous smile, and I wave my hands, jumping in before she can embarrass me further. "She was kidding. Of course, she was coming."

Ben chuckles at our sisterly banter. "Well, I'm glad you enjoyed it because I have a reservation for us to grab some wine and food."

"Perfect," Stacy cheers, giving him a playful salute. "I love a man with a plan."

The evening carries on in warm, lingering moments. At the restaurant, Ben pulls my chair out, ever attentive, and catches my gaze with a smile that conveys everything I haven't yet found the words for. We order a bottle of Pinot Noir, laughing over dinner, diving into each other's stories like old friends.

At one point, Stacy pulls out her phone, smiling as she snaps a photo of us. She's quick to type something, her grin almost conspiratorial.

"Who are you sending that to?" I ask, tilting my head with a grin.

"Cole," she says nonchalantly, still typing away.

My eyebrows shoot up in surprise. "Cole Hester? The Midnight Tide's head of security?"

Ben and I exchange curious glances, but Stacy doesn't even look up. "Well, yeah. Just thought he should know he's missing out on the fun."

"And since when have you two been texting each other?" I probe, feigning casual interest.

"Oh, you know," she shrugs. "Just whenever I'm around."

"Uh-huh. So, every month?"

"Something like that."

Her nonchalance makes me wonder if she's even aware of how much interest Cole seems to have in her. I try not to let on, but I'm enjoying this little discovery. Leaning forward, I grin. "So... are you two seeing each other?"

"No!" Stacy replies immediately, a faint blush coloring her cheeks. "We're just friends. I mean, after what we all went through on the ship last time, it's nice to have someone who understands."

She means it innocently, but her words leave a tightness in my chest. That was no ordinary experience; it was something I don't want to relive. I don't know how to tell her that without sounding overly dramatic.

Ben must sense the tension because he reaches for my hand under the table, his fingers lacing through mine, grounding me. He lowers his voice, just for me. "You okay?"

I nod, forcing a smile, though I know he can see through it. "Yes, of course."

Thankfully, Stacy, oblivious, chimes in, sparing me from any deeper thoughts. "Oh, and by the way, Cole did ask me out once."

My jaw drops, and I can't help but laugh. "What? When did this happen?"

"End of summer."

"And you're only telling me this now?"

"Well, it's not like I encouraged it," she says, shrugging as if this is no big deal. "I told him I'd think about it."

"And have you?"

Stacy lifts her chin, pretending to consider it. "Still thinking."

We both burst into laughter, a shared moment mirroring each other's cautious approach to love.

The night wraps up with Ben driving us back to my apartment, the quiet, warm glow of the city making it feel like a secret shared only among us. He lingers by the door, his hand resting on mine for just a second longer than necessary. "Tomorrow, then?" he murmurs, his eyes holding mine.

"Tomorrow," I reply softly.

Stacy and I laugh as we stumble back up to the apartment, Rex greeting us with the same boundless energy as ever. She pours us each a glass of water, her cheeks flushed with laughter. It's been a night to remember, and as I settle down, I can't help but feel a strange sense of peace, something I haven't felt in a while.

If only it could last.

Unlock the next chapter:

Visit – https://www.amazon.com/dp/B0DPNH749Y
(Piercing Shadows Book 2)

www.ingramcontent.com/pod-product-compliance
Lightning Source LLC
Chambersburg PA
CBHW070758160726
48004CB00001B/236